John C. Holbrook

Recollections of a Nonagenarian

John C. Holbrook

Recollections of a Nonagenarian

ISBN/EAN: 9783337277338

Printed in Europe, USA, Canada, Australia, Japan

Cover: Foto ©Andreas Hilbeck / pixelio.de

More available books at **www.hansebooks.com**

RECOLLECTIONS OF A NONAGENARIAN

OF

Life in New England, the Middle West, and New York,
including a Mission to Great Britain in Behalf
of the Southern Freedmen; together
with Scenes in California

BY

REV. JOHN C. HOLBROOK, D. D., LL. D.

" Sweet odors reach us yet,
Brought sweetly from the fields long left behind."

BOSTON
The Pilgrim Press
CHICAGO

REQUESTS FOR PUBLICATION

On motion of Rev. W. C. Pond, D. D., the following action was taken unanimously by the Monday Club of San Francisco and vicinity, California, July 5, 1897:

WHEREAS, It has been reported to this Club that our venerable brother, Rev. J. C. Holbrook, D. D., has yielded to the request of many friends to issue an autobiography; therefore,

Resolved, *I*, That this Monday Club of Congregational Ministers and Laymen adds its request to those already made, and rejoices that the good work done by our brother in various departments of service to Christ will have the accurate and vivid picturing which only the worker's own hand can give.

Resolved, *II*, That in our opinion that portion of his ministry in which he stood in the forefront of the contention for the right of a church and a minister to be *Congregational* without reproach and without suspicion, in the West as well as in the East, and all over the world as well as in New England, should receive special attention, to the end that the memory of those heroic pioneers, who, half a century ago, were standing for this right, may be held in due honor, and be not allowed to fade.

SOME LETTERS

Extract from a letter from Rev. G. S. F. Savage, D. D., Secretary of the Board of Directors of Chicago Theological Seminary, who has been for fifty years prominent and active in Congregational work in Illinois:

CHICAGO, July 29, 1897.

MY DEAR DR. HOLBROOK: I was much gratified with the action of the San Francisco Monday Club, urging you to prepare your autobiography. I certainly hope you will comply with the request, and that without delay. Your life has been identified with the history of our denomination in a remarkable manner for three fourths of a century; and you have had part in many notable enterprises, East and West, the record of which should be preserved.

From Rev. A. S. Kedzie, Grand Haven, Michigan, who was for fourteen years financial agent of the Chicago Theological Seminary, a corporate member and a coöperator in its establishment from the first:

I am glad to learn that you, as requested, consent to write for publication the recollections of your lifetime as a nonagenarian. Included in your book, doubtless, will be an account of Chicago Theological Seminary. You were one of the charter members, and held a seat in its Board of Directors from 1854 to 1864. During those ten years the Seminary came into life and form and place and power, developing its peculiar characteristics, wherein, during that formative period of its life, it was largely helped by your action in the Board, and also by your advocacy in the *Congregational Herald*, then edited by you, and in whose office the Board sometimes held meetings.

From Rev. S. H. Willey, D. D., one of the home missionary pioneers of California, and the founder and first pastor of the First Presbyterian Church in San Francisco.

I am glad to know your autobiography is in press. I remember once urging you to write it. It was due to you and to truth.

PREFATORY NOTE

At the earnest solicitation of some of my relatives and personal friends, including the Congregational Monday Club of San Francisco, California, I have been induced to write out some autobiographical notes and reminiscences of my life, and they are now printed, not so much for general circulation as for their pleasure. I hesitated long before complying with their request, lest I should be regarded as entertaining an undue sense of the importance of my life, and should be accused of egotism, since of necessity I should be compelled to use the personal pronoun. In the prosecution of my task I have recorded many particulars that would naturally interest those for whom I wrote, but which might be regarded as unimportant by others; and I may properly add, that should these notes seem to be self-laudatory, what I have written was necessary in order to give my friends a due conception of my life-work.

It is also proper to remark that the letters from Great Britain, from which I have given copious extracts, were mostly written to my wife, who naturally desired to learn how I was received there, and what were the results of my mission to that country. If, therefore, this volume should fall into the hands of persons outside of the circle for which it was prepared, they will please bear in mind for whom and for what purpose it was written.

J. C. H.

Stockton, California.

CONTENTS

CHAPTER VI

CHAPTER VII

CHAPTER VIII

CHAPTER IX

CHAPTER X

CHAPTER XVII

CHAPTER XVIII

CHAPTER XIX

CHAPTER XX

CHAPTER XXI

CHAPTER XXII

CHAPTER XXIII

CHAPTER XXXI

CHAPTER XXXII

CHAPTER XXXIII

CHAPTER XXXIV

CHAPTER XXXV

CHAPTER XXXVI

Recollections of a Nonagenarian

CHAPTER I

BIRTH AND PARENTAGE—BOYHOOD—SCHOOLS
—MILITARY ACADEMY

The century through nearly the whole of which I have lived, may be regarded, in many respects, as the most remarkable of any in the history of the world. I began life near the close of Jefferson's administration as president of the United States, and have therefore lived under every president save two. And it is a notable fact, illustrative of the exceeding brevity of our nation's history, that my father's life and my own together outspan that history by several years. My father was born in Weymouth, Massachusetts, near Boston, in 1763, or thirteen years before the Declaration of Independence, and twenty-five before the adoption of the Constitution that transformed the thirteen original colonies into a nation. He recollected distinctly the excitement caused by the battles of Concord and Lexington, and could almost have heard " the shot that," as Emerson says, " was heard around the world." I have a book containing the Holbrook genealogy, that shows that my father was a direct descendant of Governor Bradford of Plymouth colony, his great-great-grandmother having been Welthea Bradford, daughter of the governor.

But brief as has been the existence of the United States as a nation, yet how wonderful has been its growth from a few feeble confederate, local organizations to a place among the foremost nations of the earth, and from three millions of people to over seventy millions! Of much of this progress I have been a witness, together with many events, secular and religious, that have characterized this century now about to end.

I first saw the light January 7, 1808, according to my father's family record, in Brattleboro, in the state of Vermont, one of the most beautiful villages in our land. It is situated on the west bank of the lovely Connecticut river, the largest stream in New England, and in the midst of the most romantic scenery. A mountain peak one thousand feet high overlooks it from the opposite shore of the river, at whose foot the stream winds its tortuous way. To the west are the foot-hills of the Green Mountains, and on the north, the fine, fertile meadows through which the West river, that rises in the mountains to the northwest, flows to its junction with the larger stream. Beyond these meadows is seen a range of very picturesque hills, the place chosen by Rudyard Kipling, the novelist, for his abode, and from which the village is in full view. The first President Dwight of Yale College, in his published account of his journey by carriage, many years ago, from New Haven to Canada, says that the view of the village and its surroundings which burst upon him from Prospect or Cemetery Hill, as he approached from the south, was the most entrancing that he had ever witnessed.

My mother was born in Shrewsbury, Massachusetts, and was the daughter of Judge Luke Knowlton, who emigrated to Newfane, Vermont, while she was young, where afterwards she was married to my father. She was of a remarkably cheerful, hopeful, and vivacious temperament, and from her I

2

inherited much of those characteristics, and from her I received religious influences that have abided with me through life. Her piety was deep and sincere, and her prayers have helped to shape my life. I had no doubt that she desired from the first that I should become a minister of the gospel, and her prayers to that effect, though the answer was delayed a while, were at last answered, and for that I shall ever be grateful to her and to Him who answers prayer. I never lost the impression of her fervid devotions as she conducted family worship in the absence of my father, and one favorite petition has always dwelt in my mind as she used to utter it from her heart, " Draw us by the cords of Thy love, and we shall run after Thee." What an unspeakable blessing has been my heritage from such godly parents as were mine !

My brother, ex-Governor Holbrook of Vermont, learning that I was preparing this work, sent me the following tribute to our mother :

She was a superior woman in many respects; a great beauty in person and of talented mind, and had the gift of imagination, as well as reasoning powers. She was very fond of poetry. and retained much of it through life. I have heard her repeat whole paragraphs, and

once a long passage from " The Lady of the Lake," and
in her last days I read much of such literature to her.
She was quite a theologian, and in long and heated argu-
ments would get the better of our father. She was more
thoroughly balanced in mind than he, and less affected
by prejudice. He was a very strong man, and of stern
piety, but subject to prejudices that sometimes warped
his judgment.

Referring to her personal appearance, my
father used to relate that, when a young man,
he was once at her father's house on business,
when suddenly the door of the room opened
and a young woman appeared, with flashing
black eyes, and round, ruddy face, and he
found himself captured for life. It was love
at first sight; those remarkably bright eyes,
which were a marked feature, sent an irresistible dart to his heart.

I spent my early boyhood in Brattleboro,
drinking in the pure and invigorating air of
the Green Mountain state, to which, no doubt,
I owe in part my longevity, so much beyond
the period usually allotted to man. At first
I attended the district school, and there acquired the rudiments of education. Well do I
remember the stern visage of the tall teacher,
who might well have stood as the original of
Goldsmith's celebrated pedagogue, in regard
to whom the people " wondered how one

small head could carry all he knew." He was a most rigid disciplinarian, and resorted to measures to enforce his rule which were peculiar, and which could hardly be imitated at the present day.

One of these was the compelling of a guilty boy to sit on a front seat between two girls. Another was, to place such a one on a table in the middle of the room, to stand on one leg as long as he could endure it, and then change to the other, alternately. Then there was an immense fireplace, closed in the summer by a fireboard, and it was a favorite mode of punishment to put a refractory boy inside for meditation and until he should repent. One boy, it was said, on such an occasion climbed up the chimney and came out at the top. Another, when he came out, caused an uproarious laugh, as he had made a blackamoor of himself with the soot on his hands and face. What progress I made in learning in this primitive school I do not distinctly remember, but I think it was not much, as I was then an active boy and more fond of play than of books.

I was early impressed with the deep and earnest piety of my parents. Family worship was regularly conducted by my father or, in his absence, as I have said, by my mother. The Sabbath was strictly observed, and the whole family attended public worship. I had five sisters older than myself, and all were professed Christians. I remember that the Congregational house of worship, of the old-fashioned style of architecture, " two stories in height, painted white, and abounding in windows above and below, with a tall spire," stood on the bleakest spot on the common, and was furnished with no means for heating, and there the audience sat shivering for two hours, the frequent length of the services. My brother, to whom I have already referred, four years my junior, in some reminiscences of the time, prepared at the request of the present pastor of the church, thus alludes to those services :

The gallery at the end opposite the pulpit was occupied by the singers, consisting of some thirty or forty persons of both sexes. There was no instrument but a violincello and flute, and the old fugue tunes were in fashion. Through these the choir used to *tear* at the top of their voices, the audience thinking them grand and inspiring. I remember how startling some of old Dr. Watts's hymns used to sound with all the ringing changes and repetitions of the fugue movement, each part taking up one line after the other, and chasing each other till they all came out finally to-gether on the last line. I remember some of these hymns :

> "Lord, what a thoughtless wretch was I," etc.
> "Hark from the tombs, a doleful sound," etc.

Among the ministers who supplied the pulpit by exchange with the pastor, was Rev. Dr. Taggart of Colerain. Massachusetts, a Scotchman, a very strong and able man and preacher, and who at one period represented his district in Congress, and when his party wished, for any reason, to gain time, they depended on him to speak, as he could do for a whole day or more, on any question. His sermons were from an hour to an hour and a half long, and extended frequently to sixteenthly, and the different divisions were introduced by the phrase, "Ah! but furder." He used to pray with his eyes wide open, and they would follow persons coming late, clear to their pews near the pulpit, he looking down to see that they were properly located, his· prayer going on straight and regular. I remember one favorite passage which he used often, that "Zion might be beautiful as Tirza and comely as Jerusalem, and terrible as an army with banners." We boys could not comprehend wherein banners were terrible, as shooting-irons we knew were. He was usually a guest at my father's house, and in conducting family worship he stood with his hands resting on the back of a chair, facing the front windows of the room, and as the horses with sleigh-bells passed by on the street, he would lean forward and follow them with his eyes till they were out of sight, his prayer going on uninterruptedly.

One of the early recollections of my youth was the appearance at my father's table one day, of Obookiah, a young native of the Sandwich Islands. He had been brought to New Haven by a sea captain, and one day he was discovered sitting on the door-step of one of the college buildings and weeping bitterly because there was no one to instruct him. This led to the establishment of a mission school at Cornwall, Connecticut, where he was sent, and led to the subsequent despatch of missionaries by our American Board of Commissioners for Foreign Missions, to those islands, and to their evangelization. Obookiah, however, died in this country. At the time I referred to, he, with one of the teachers, I think, of the school passed through my native place, and were guests of my father's house, and was an object of great interest among Christians. At the time of the visit referred to, there happened to be at my father's a literary gentleman from Boston, who expressed afterwards great indignation that he was compelled to sit at the same dinner table with a colored man!

After leaving the district school I became a pupil in a private school, kept by the governess of the children of my widowed eldest sister and those of a few friends. There I made decided progress under her genial influence. After this I was transferred, at about the age of twelve, to Hopkins Academy, in Old Hadley, Massachusetts, a quaint old town, mostly built on one street, a mile long and nearly a quarter of a mile wide, the space between the two sides covered with grass, on which every family had the right to pasture a flock of geese. In the middle of the street, equidistant from each end, stood the white Congregational church building, with its tall spire. In early days the men used to carry their muskets to church in view of a possible attack by the Indians. It was in this town that the regicide Whalley was concealed in a house near the church, after the death of Charles I. When on one Sunday there was an attack by the Indians, he suddenly appeared on the scene and led the defense and put the foe to flight by waving his sword, the Indians believing him to be a supernatural being.

The principal of the academy was the Rev. Dan Huntington, father of Bishop Huntington of Central New York. He was a very dignified and awe-inspiring man, and strict in government, while his assistant, a middle-aged lawyer, was exactly the opposite, and by far the more popular with the school. The institution had a high repute among the few of that kind then in existence, with a male and female department.

There I began fitting for college, intending to enter Yale or Middlebury, and there I acquired some knowledge of Latin and Greek. The building was afterwards burned and never rebuilt, as there was another institution of the kind at Amherst, seven miles distant, which presented more attractions for pupils. I was a student at Hopkins academy for two years, and there I was associated with Jeremiah Porter, afterwards well known as the founder of the first church in Chicago, while he was chaplain to the United States army post at Fort Dearborn.

Leaving Hopkins Academy, I was under the tutelage for a year of Rev. Ephraim H. Newton of Marlboro, Vermont, a neighboring town to my native place. He was a scholarly man, and very fond of mineralogy, and was afterwards made a D. D., and became pastor of the Presbyterian church in Glenns Falls, New York. Here I was associated with Alvan Tobey, afterwards a distinguished minister in New Hampshire. Mr. Newton was very helpful to me, and took me into his family.

In 1819 Capt. Alden Partridge resigned his position as superintendent of the U. S. Military Academy at West Point, and established in his native town of Norwich, Vermont,

system, and in after life it was remarked of me that my erect form and military step indicated that I had seen service.

Says Hon. Luther R. Marsh, an eminent New York lawyer, once connected with the institution :

It was most useful to its students, that while it afforded the advanced means of that day for education, it straightened up and gave elasticity to the cadets, settled their constitutions, induced habits of walking through country roads, and established a physique to endure the strain of competition in after life.

The same writer gives the following sketch of the life of the founder, Capt. Alden Partridge :

He was graduated at West Point in 1806, and was commissioned as first lieutenant in the corps of engineers and assistant professor of mathematics. In 1810 he became captain, and in 1813 professor of mathematics and engineering, and, for a time, was superintendent of the West Point institution. He afterwards took charge of the survey for exploring our northwestern boundary under the treaty of Ghent. Subsequently, he founded the military school at Norwich, Vermont, and became surveyor-general of that state. In 1825 he closed the school at Norwich and opened it at Middletown. He was afterwards a member of the Vermont legislature. In 1840 he founded several other military schools in different states.

He was famous as a pedestrian. In one of his excursions, he accomplished seventy miles in a single day.

CHAPTER II

At the end of my course at the military
school, my father, who was advancing in
years, became desirous of retiring from business, and wished me to be prepared to take
his place. He accordingly introduced me as
a clerk in the establishment in which he was
associated as a partner with my brother-in-
law, Mr. Joseph Fessenden, under the firm
name of Holbrook & Fessenden. They were
engaged in the manufacture of paper and
books in my native place, Brattleboro, and
were well known not only in all New England, but in the country at large. The business had been started about the beginning of
this century, by another brother-in-law of
mine who had died, the husband of my
oldest sister, Mr. William Fessenden. They
published a great variety of miscellaneous
works, among which I remember the then
very popular " Scottish Chiefs," " Rasselas "

by Dr. Johnson, " Hervey's Meditations," then much read, and many other works then standard, but now almost forgotten. They employed peddlers, who traversed New England, selling books and paper, or exchanging them for rags for the paper-mill and sheep skins for the bindery, and dry goods for the supply of the men and women in their employ.

They also published the famous spelling-book of Noah Webster, then almost exclusively used in this country, of which they issued 100,000 copies per annum, and many millions in all, as, with one or two other houses, they had the exclusive right of publication. They were sent in boxes, for wholesale trade, to New York and the Southern cities. My father, also, had purchased a set of stereotype plates of the quarto Bible, the first ever used in this country, which had been imported from England. From these the firm issued an elegant, illustrated quarto family Bible, which was sold by subscription at $12 a copy, and which had a wide circulation.

Thus it will be seen that a position of no small importance was presented to me, and one in which I had the opportunity to acquire a valuable amount of knowledge of business. As there was a large circulating library in the store, I also became familiar with general literature, which was afterwards of great value to me in my professional life. I also, at this time, studied the French language, in a class taught by an educated *émigré* from France, who came to reside for a time in the place.

CHAPTER III

POLITICS—CONVERSION, AND ENTRANCE ON THE CHRISTIAN LIFE

While serving as a clerk in the book business, I was applied to by the proprietor of the village newspaper, who was not an educated man, to write his leading editorials, and in performing this duty I became interested in politics. It was the period of the great excitement connected with the contest for the presidency of the United States between General Jackson and John Quincy Adams for his second term, and the controversies following the election of the former, in regard to his course generally, and especially as to the national bank. I adopted the Whig platform, advocated the claims of Adams, and opposed the measures of Jackson. At this election I made my first and only bet, that of a hat, that Adams would win, and of course I lost it.

I attended conventions, and at one of them delivered an elaborate speech, which was printed and attracted some attention. In fact, had I gone on in that direction, I have reason to believe I might have achieved some success as a politician, and possibly have acquired office. But God had other and better designs in regard to me, for which I can never be too thankful. There was no political position that I could possibly have obtained, that, had I my life to live over again, I would prefer to that which I have had the privilege to occupy as a minister of the gospel.

As I have said, God had something better for me than a political career, and by a marked interposition changed my whole future course in life. It was an event never to be forgotten, either in this world or the next. There occurred one of those precious seasons to which so many trace their entrance on a Christian life, a revival of religion in the Congregational church. I attended the meetings, and the conviction I had before entertained was deepened, that I ought to be a Christian. I knew I was the subject of prayer on the part of my friends, and especially of my pious mother, and I began inquiring what I ought to do to become a Christian. But I was perplexed, as no specific directions were given, as there should have been.

At length, on one Sabbath afternoon,—how well I remember the very time and place!—I sat in my chamber reading "Doddridge's Rise and Progress of Religion in the Soul," when I came upon a chapter in which he recommends the making of a specific consecration of one's self to God, and gives a form to be written out and adopted. At once it flashed upon me that I had never done this, and instantly kneeling down by my bedside, with the book open before me, I adopted the form set forth, and prayed that God would accept the dedication for Christ's sake. Then rising, I believed that he did ratify the transaction, and that henceforth I was to be a servant of Jesus Christ and no longer my own, and from that day to this, for more than threescore and ten years, I have sought to serve him. Then and there my whole character and course of life were changed; I at once entered upon the discharge of Christian duties as they came to me, and ever since it has been my prayer,—

> Oh, may thy Spirit guide my feet
> In ways of righteousness,
> Make every path of duty straight,
> And plain before my face.

I soon applied for admission to the church, and in due time was received to membership. Later I was elected superintendent of the Sunday-school, and a deacon in connection with my father,—a somewhat peculiar case.

CHAPTER IV

ENTRANCE ON BUSINESS, AND MARRIAGE

After I had finished my apprenticeship of a few years in business, my father retired, and I became his successor in the firm of Holbrook & Fessenden. I have ever regarded the experience thus gained in business as of great value to me in my subsequent professional life as a minister of the gospel. It gave me a knowledge of men and of the world which so many lack who go directly from the college and seminary into the ministry. It enabled me to understand the views and feelings of the laity in regard to the functions of the pastor; and, as I have before said, it led me to the cultivation of a literary taste; and it made me more of a *practical* man in my after profession than I should otherwise have been, and less of a mere theorist.

Soon after beginning my business career, I entered upon the family state also. I became acquainted with Miss Cynthia S. Tuttle of Windsor, Vermont, a niece and ward of Hon. William Page of Rutland, Vermont, and we were married at his house, January 12, 1829. There were born to us four children, —three sons and one daughter. The two youngest died in early childhood, and were buried in the family lot in Prospect Hill cemetery, in Brattleboro. The other two rest with their mother in the soil of Iowa. The eldest, a son, lived to be nineteen.

I continued in business in my native place for several years, and was an active member of the church. I remember especially a very powerful revival of religion, in which I was much interested, that occurred during that period. A celebrated revivalist labored in the church, and there was a large number of conversions, including many of the prominent citizens of the place.

During the period of which I have been writing, I had an opportunity to put in practice the military knowledge I had acquired at the military academy. I was appointed aide-de-camp to the brigadier-general of militia, and as I had seen service, he depended on me to assist and advise in the discharge of his duties. It was the time when general "musters" were in fashion, when all the able-bodied men of military age were required to appear and answer to their names, and to be drilled and inspected. There were a few independent companies in uniform, both infantry and cavalry, that made a respectable show, but the rank and file (called "the floodwood") generally appeared in their ordinary dress, with all kinds of arms, and sometimes with none, or displaying canes and poles as a substitute, and they made a very grotesque appearance. There was usually a sham fight near the close of the day. Crowds of men and women, and especially of boys, were in attendance as spectators on such occasions, while hucksters drove a thriving business in gingerbread, small beer, crackers, and lemonade, and sometimes, I am sorry to say, in stronger drinks. There was not, however, much drunkenness, after all, and the day passed off with great delight, especially to the boys.

CHAPTER V

REMOVAL TO BOSTON—OLD BOOKSELLERS—
DR. LYMAN BEECHER AND HIS WORK—
THE UNITARIAN CONTROVERSY—LITERARY
MEN—TWO GREAT WORKS

After being in business several years in my native place, I disposed of my interest there to my partner and brother-in-law, and removed to Boston. The senior partner in one of the oldest and most extensive bookselling and publishing houses, Mr. Richardson, of the firm of Richardson & Lord, had died, and I was offered the opportunity of succeeding him, as I did, purchasing his share in the business. It had been begun, about the close of the last century, by John West, and then followed the firm of West & Richardson; then Richardson & Lord, and finally Richardson, Lord & Holbrook. We had a large jobbing trade with country merchants and booksellers, and were importers of stationery and publishers of books, and, of course, had dealings with other booksellers in other cities. We had the almost exclusive issue of books

of church music then in general use, including the works of the well-known Lowell Ma-
son, Mus. D., and the Handel & Haydn
Society of Boston, both of which had a very
extensive sale. We also published Pierpont's
series of school readers, then in very general
use, and the old Farmer's Almanac, by Robert
B. Thomas, of which we sold a hundred thousand a year. It was very popular, as it fore-
told the weather!

My position in Boston brought me in con-
tact with many authors, including Mr. Samuel
G. Goodrich, the original "Peter Parley,"
who at that time was in the habit of employ-
ing promising young men as hack writers of
books to which his real or assumed name
was attached, and in this way most of the
very popular "Peter Parley" books were prepared. Among these writers I remember
John and Epes Sargent, afterwards well
known, and no less a man than Nathaniel
Hawthorne, who had not then entered upon
his great career. John Pierpont, the poet,
and pastor of Hollis-street Unitarian church,
some of whose books we published, and other
writers were often in our place of business.
John Quincy Adams was one, a Fourth of
July oration of whose we once published.

Of course I was familiar with all the old booksellers of the day,—Samuel T. Armstrong, Crocker & Brewster, Hilliard, Gray & Co., Hilliard, Little & Brown, William T. Ticknor, and Carter & Hendee,—all of whom, including my partner, Mr. Melvin Lord, have passed away. I knew, also, the old booksellers of other cities. It was the custom then to hold trade sales by catalogue, in Philadelphia, the leading houses contributing their publications and being represented, and purchasing those of other houses. It was a grand wholesale auction and exchange, and I sometimes attended. We usually closed the occasion with a grand banquet. There was generally a large attendance of those in the trade. The old building we occupied, adjoining Ticknor's, near the corner of Washington and School streets, is still standing.

On removing to Boston, I united with the church of which old Dr. Lyman Beecher was the pastor, and I acted as clerk of the church for a time. Dr. Beecher was then in the very zenith of his power and fame as a preacher, and there were continual conversions. In one revival, I remember, he was assisted by Dr. N. W. Taylor of New Haven, a man of great power as a preacher. They were bosom friends, having been intimate when Dr. Beecher was settled in Litchfield, Connecticut, and they were in entire harmony in their religious views, with which I also sympathized. I have always considered my connection with that church as almost equivalent to a course in a theological seminary. It was a part of God's appointed preparation of me for my subsequent professional career.

Dr. Beecher's call to Boston was one of the measures of the friends of orthodoxy for counteracting the influence of Unitarianism, of which Dr. Channing was then the leader, and the air was full of the controversy. Dr. Enoch Pond, the father of Rev. Dr. W. C. Pond of San Francisco, was then editing that spicy monthly, *The Spirit of the Pilgrims*, and Dr. Beecher aided him. I remember a very lively tilt of Dr. Beecher with the editor of the leading Unitarian paper, in reference to the salvation of infants, in which the doctor was at his best in sarcasm, and there was no little excitement in religious circles. The doctor closed by recommending to his antagonist to study the commandment against bearing false witness against his neighbor. His opponent had quoted every statement of ultra Calvinists of past ages and applied them to

Congregationalists of the present day, and as they were not accepted then, he was charged with bearing false witness.

At this time occurred, also, the great controversy in regard to the preaching of the famous revivalist, Charles G. Finney. The doctor had embraced some of the erroneous statements against Mr. Finney, but he afterwards abandoned them and heartily coöperated with him in a series of meetings in Boston.

The power of Dr. Beecher's eloquence was very great in the pulpit. He was in the habit of using a brief, instead of a fully-written sermon, and he would occasionally glance down on his paper and catch a point, and then, throwing up his spectacles to the top of his head, pour out a volume of eloquence that would thrill the audience like a stroke of electricity. When we saw the glasses go up, we were on the alert, for we then expected something that would be well worth hearing and remembering.

President Sturtevant, in his autobiography, says he once administered the Lord's Supper in Dr. Beecher's church in Cincinnati, when the doctor was unwell, and at the close Mr. S. asked him to say a few words, "when Dr.

Beecher rose," says Mr. S., "and poured forth from his overflowing soul, for nearly half an hour, the most magnificent strain of evangelic eloquence I have ever heard." During the evening, Mr. S. asked the doctor how he had acquired that perfectly easy and natural tone that invariably characterized his delivery. He instantly replied, "I didn't acquire it, for I always had it." "Just so." says Mr. S., '*poeta nascitur, non fit*.' "

At this time, and under these influences, my former conviction that I ought to preach the gospel was renewed and deepened, and I then seriously contemplated giving up business and entering on a course of preparation for it. I even went so far as to open a correspondence with Dr. Porter, the president of Andover Theological Seminary, with a view to entering that institution as a special student. But this did not approve itself to some of my relatives, and the idea was abandoned for the time.

My thoughts at this period were much occupied with religious matters. Then it was that I devised the plan of the "Comprehensive Commentary on the Bible," a combination of the Expositions of Matthew Henry and Thomas Scott abridged, with that of Dr. Doddridge, with all of which I was familiar, together with notes, additional, original, and selected. Then, also, I conceived the plan of the " Encyclopedia of Religious Knowledge," on the basis of "Buck's Theological Dictionary," with large additions of other matter, biographical and illustrative of the Scriptures, forming a large royal octavo volume, of which, I have been told, a hundred thousand copies have been sold.

At length I determined to dispose of my interest in the Boston establishment and return to my native place and resume my position there, and to publish these works by subscription. Having engaged Rev. William Jenks, D. D., an eminent scholar, as editor, with an assistant for doing the abridging, and Rev. J. Newton Brown to edit the Encyclopedia, I returned to Brattleboro and put my plan in execution.

CHAPTER VI

Returning then to my native place, I became an active member of the church, and a deacon and Sunday-school superintendent. But the old and persistent idea that I ought to preach the gospel continued in full force in my mind, and, notwithstanding the cares of business, I devoted time to the study of theology, mastering Dr. Dwight's system among other works, and giving special attention to the subject of baptism, on which my mind had become somewhat disturbed; but after careful examination I became fully satisfied with our Congregational views of the matter. For a considerable time I was in the habit of practising lay preaching, in a schoolhouse in one of the outlying districts of the parish, holding a service in the late afternoon. I also once contemplated applying to the Ministerial Association of the

county for approbation as a preacher, and
Rev. Dr. Jenks wrote a very flattering recommendation in my favor, but it was never
presented, and no steps were taken in that
direction.

At this time, also, I became much interested in the cause of temperance, and engaged Mr. O. S. Fowler, afterwards celebrated as a phrenologist, then a student in
Amherst College, to canvass the county and
distribute temperance publications, making
my house his headquarters. While thus
employed, he wrote and delivered in the village his first lecture on his favorite topic,
"Phrenology." At his recommendation also,
I invited his friend and classmate, Henry
Ward Beecher, to come and lecture on temperance in the village. Mr. Beecher accordingly came, and spoke in the hall of the High
School, and was my guest. This was his
first appearance as a public speaker, and he
always said that I first introduced him to
public life.

Mr. Beecher was fond of referring to this
in after life, and once, when I was present at
one of his week evening meetings in Brooklyn, he related the circumstance, and indicated me as having first brought him out

as a public speaker. He wrote once for a periodical an amusing account of his experience at that time. He said that for want of money he walked all the way from Amherst to Brattleboro, forty miles, and then walked back again, as I had carelessly neglected to pay him for his services. But a few days after there came a letter to him from me, enclosing a ten dollar bank note, the first money he ever earned, and then he was at a great loss how to invest it. He was greatly excited by the possession of so much money, and finally resolved to go up to the book-store and perhaps buy out the stock. He accordingly went there and surveyed the array of books, but concluded he could not secure the whole, and so he finally bought what he could with his money, and with the package under his arm returned to his room, the proudest and richest man in the town. He never forgot this experience, and often referred to it in conversation with me after he had achieved fame.

It was during my second residence in my native place that the legislature of the state made an appropriation of $3,000 for the survey of a railroad route from the south line of the state up the west side of the Connecticut river, and the governor appointed me as a commissioner to superintend the expenditure. I engaged Professor Twining of New Haven for the work, which he accomplished; and this, if I am not mistaken, was the first railroad survey in the state.

About this time, also, a benevolent widow in Hinsdale, New Hampshire, adjoining Brattleboro, died and left a legacy of $10,000 for founding an Asylum for the Insane in Brattleboro, and made me one of four trustees for executing the bequest. The other trustees were Hon. Samuel Clark, E. Seymour, and my father. They were all very cautious business men, of a conservative spirit, and advanced in life, and they were very decided in the opinion that nothing could be done with so small a sum. But I was younger, and naturally of a very hopeful temperament, and I insisted that there should be a beginning, and that application should be made to the state for aid, and that perhaps other individuals would contribute additional funds. I find the following reference to the subject in the volume, "Annals of the Insane Asylum," by the superintendent:

It was a current remark by citizens and business men, that a failure would be the probable result of an undertaking so slenderly endowed. There is evidence that the other three members of the Board of Trustees doubted the expediency of attempting to carry out the provisions of the will. To Mr. John C. Holbrook (the junior member) is undoubtedly due the credit of assuming, at this juncture, in earnest, the work necessary to inaugurate the enterprise, which his energy and sanguine temperament fitted him especially for.

It was finally decided to make a beginning. I was appointed secretary of the board, and began an extensive correspondence with persons of experience and those who would naturally be interested in the object. Among these was Rev. Lewis Dwight of the Prison Discipline Society, who heartily entered into the enterprise, and afforded valuable advice and assistance. He introduced me to Dr. Julius, a German philanthropist, then in this country, who had given attention to the relief of the insane.

It was finally decided to apply to the legislature for an act of incorporation and a grant of money. The act was passed, and a small appropriation made, which was ultimately increased to $10,000. A very fine site for the institution was purchased, after a careful examination of the vicinity of the village, which site was subsequently greatly enlarged. The services of Dr. W. H. Rockwell were secured as superintendent. He had been trained by the celebrated Dr. Todd, of the Insane Retreat at Hartford, Connecticut, and had been an assistant there. In this we were very fortunate, for Dr. Rockwell proved a most valuable and successful manager, and to him is certainly owing the great success of the institution. Under him the buildings were erected and enlarged from time to time, and great additions were made to the real estate.

When this asylum was first opened, there were but nine such in the United States. Rev. Mr. Dwight, to whom I have referred, wrote me,—

So far as my observation extends (and his observation was wide), there is not a more beautiful spot of earth than that which you have secured for the Vermont asylum. Those at Charlestown and Worcester, Mass., and at Hartford and Bloomingdale bear no comparison to it. It is difficult to convey an adequate idea of the beauty of the grounds and surrounding hills. English medical superintendents should supply the defect of my description by a personal visit.

For the first two or three years, in addition to my extensive correspondence, I wrote the reports of the institution for the legislature and the applications for aid, setting forth the necessity for providing for the relief of the unfortunates deprived of reason.

My brother, ex-Governor Holbrook of Vermont, who has been for many years a trustee of the institution, and has had the superintendence of the agricultural and horticultural department, writes me, under date July 29, 1897, as follows:

The Vermont Asylum for the Insane, now called the Brattleboro Retreat, until about two years ago took in all Vermont insane patients, from 450 to 500 in number. But to accommodate so many would require considerable enlargement, which the trustees did not consider advisable, and they therefore recommended to the state authorities to provide for a portion of the state patients elsewhere. The legislature, therefore, appropriated *five hundred thousand* dollars for a state institution at Waterbury, and there most of the patients supported by the state are cared for.

The Brattleboro Retreat now owns about eight hundred acres of land contiguous to the institution, being one of the best farms in the valley of the Connecticut. A large vegetable garden supplies all the luxuries of the season in that line, and fifty cows furnish abundance of milk. A large park of forty acres, with numerous walks, affords a place for recreation and exercise for the patients. And all this, including the state institution, is the result of the modest bequest of $10,000 by Mrs. Marsh. I have been thus full on this subject, because I count my agency in the matter as one of the important transactions of my life.

I am thankful, indeed, that my faith that Mrs. Marsh's little "grain of mustard seed," if planted and cared for, would develop into "a tree, in whose branches the birds of the air might rest," was not vain. But this is only one of a multitude of illustrations which history affords, that, in the providence of God, vast and beneficial results have flowed from what seemed to human eyes very insignificant beginnings. Let us not "despise the day of small things." No benevolent act, however small, is performed in vain, and we may confidently expect the blessing of God on any enterprise undertaken for His glory and the good of mankind.

CHAPTER VII

After a time, it was found that private capital was inadequate to meet the expense of the editing, stereotyping, and publishing of such large works as we had undertaken, and it was decided to form an association and secure an act of incorporation under the title of "The Brattleboro Typographical Company." This was done, and the business was transferred accordingly, I serving for a time as president. But at length I resolved to relinquish the book business and remove to the West, where I had a brother-in-law engaged in agricultural pursuits, who was anxious that I should join him. Accordingly, with my wife and two sons, I removed to Davenport, Iowa, on the Mississippi river.

I found there only a small Presbyterian church, with a rigid, old-school pastor. At first I attended his church, and engaged in the Sabbath-school, but soon found the pastor to be an autocrat, of a domineering spirit, who insisted on controlling everything, including the Sabbath-school, in the most arbitrary manner, and, becoming disgusted, I, with a few others like-minded with myself, formed a Congregational church, in which I was elected a deacon.

I soon found I was not adapted to agricultural pursuits, and the old propensity to preach, which had followed me all my days, returned with redoubled force; and I applied to the Congregational Association, and received approbation as a minister of the gospel after a careful examination. I was recommended as a candidate for the pastorate of the church in Burlington, then the largest town in the territory of Iowa, and an appointment was made for me to preach there the following Sabbath. But before the time arrived, I was summoned home by sickness in my family, and could not fill the appointment. Had I done so, I might have settled there instead of in the place that finally became my field of labor. I found on returning home that my second son was very ill, and he soon after died. Not long after this, I received a commission from the Home Missionary society at New York, and began preaching at one or two points in the vicinity of my residence.

But I was speedily called to endure another severe affliction in the death of my wife. Our union had been a comparatively short one, of some twelve years, mostly spent amid the comforts and refinements of New England. My wife was of a slender constitution, ill adapted to the new life of the West, and, moreover, she had inherited the seeds of consumption, which soon resulted in death. She had been a devoted Christian from her youth, and passed peacefully away in the faith of the gospel, and was buried beside our son in the cemetery at Davenport. Thus I was left with only my eldest son, and my thoughts naturally turned to my old home and to the friends left there, and under the influence of a strong attack of *nostalgia*, I resolved to return to the East. But such was not the will of God. He had been preparing me for a life-work different from that I anticipated, and in part for this purpose broke up my family.

And now occurred, in accordance with His plans, one of the most remarkable providential interpositions in my affairs, of which I have so many to record, and which changed

my whole subsequent course of life. Just as
I had come to the determination to return to
New England, my family physician, Dr.
Joseph W. Clark, afterwards so well known
in San Francisco as a deacon and trustee of
the First Congregational church there, decided to seek a new field for the practice of
his profession, and for that purpose was going
with his horse and buggy to Wisconsin. He
invited me to take a seat with him, and as it
would give me an opportunity to see more of
the country, I accepted, *but without the least
idea of settling again anywhere in the West.*

We journeyed up the beautiful Rock river
valley to Beloit, and from thence proceeded
to Milwaukee, where we spent the Sabbath,
and I preached for the Rev. Dr. J. J. Miter,
in the Congregational church. There we
met Rev. Stephen Peet, the agent of the American Home Missionary Society, who was just
setting out on a trip across the state to the
Mississippi river, and he proposed that we
should accompany him. This we did, he
with his horse and buggy, and we with ours.
We had not proceeded far before we were
overtaken by one of the severest of snow-
storms, which rendered it impossible to continue on wheels. We therefore purchased a

light two-horse sled, and putting our vehicles on it, and hitching our horses together, we mounted on top of the load, and pursued our way till we reached Platteville, in the south-west corner of the state. Here the doctor decided to settle, and parting from us, he returned home. He soon after removed, with his father's family, to that place. Before doing so, however, he was married to my niece, Miss Jane W. Fessenden, who had been residing with me. Subsequently, I also married his sister.

And here I am reminded of the only joke I ever knew the doctor to perpetrate, as he was of a staid and quiet spirit. On settling in Platteville, he united with, and became an active member of, the Congregational church there, and became deeply interested in its affairs. When later, Mr. Peet, the Home Missionary agent, called on him there, the doctor began to upbraid him for not visiting the place oftener. "Oh, but," said the agent, "I wrote you often." "Yes," replied the doctor, "your letters truly were weighty and powerful, but your bodily presence was weak and contemptible."

CHAPTER VIII

As Mr. Peet, the Home Missionary agent, was going further to Potosi, on the Mississippi river, he proposed that I should accompany him, not with any view on his part or mine that I should remain in the region. Having no plan to hinder, I accepted the invitation. On our arrival at Potosi, we were requested to spend a little time there and hold a series of revival meetings; and we did so. Towards the end of the week the agent informed me that he had an appointment to preach on the following Sunday at Dubuque, Iowa, a few miles below, and on the opposite side of the Mississippi, the church there being under his care; and he suggested that I should go there in his stead. I assented, and on Sunday preached, and on the next morning before I left, I received an official " call " to the pastorate of the church, on a salary of $600, of which $200 was to come from the Home Missionary society in New York. This was to me a total surprise, as I had thought, as I have said, of nothing of the kind. I replied that I would take the matter into consideration, and returned to Potosi.

On rejoining the agent, I told him I had concluded to accept the call, at which he was as much surprised as I had been at receiving it, as he had had no such design in regard to me. Dubuque was then a godless place and far from being attractive in itself to an ambitious man ; and when the agent, on his return to Milwaukee, reported my decision to Rev. Dr. Miter, the latter expressed his astonishment also, and added (for he was something of a phrenologist), " Well, when he was here I noticed that he had the bump of hope largely developed." How marked the providence that thus changed my plans for my future life, after I had, as I supposed, definitely decided on returning to New England ! It illustrates the proverb, " Man proposes, but God disposes," or, as Shakespeare has it,—

> There's a divinity that shapes our ends,
> Rough-hew them as we will.

At that time Iowa was a territory, recently set off from Wisconsin, which had been just erected into a state. The total population of the territory did not exceed fifty thousand, occupying a narrow strip of country on the west bank of the Mississippi river, north of Missouri. There was not then a single organized state or territory west to the Pacific Ocean, nor north to the British possessions. Texas had not then been admitted to the Union, nor had the Mexican war occurred which resulted in the cession to the United States of New Mexico, Arizona, and all the vast region west of the Rocky mountains, including the present great state of California. Fremont had not then accomplished his famous exploring expedition to find a practicable route for emigrants to Oregon. In fact, the whole country westward of Iowa was an unexplored region, including a supposed immense desert, and there was not a settled minister of the gospel to the north or west of me when I went to Dubuque.

Two or three years after this, I was invited by the captain of a steamer on the Mississippi, who was going to carry supplies to the frontier United States Fort Snelling, some three hundred and fifty miles north of Dubuque, to take the trip with him. As we proceeded up the river, we did not find a single white settlement north of Iowa. At Redwing, in what is now Minnesota, we landed to visit a *foreign* missionary station among the Indians, belonging to the American Board of Foreign Missions in Boston. Proceeding on our way, we reached the fort, and I preached on board the boat on Sunday. The next day, visiting a village of Sioux Indians near by, I found it in a state of great excitement over the body of a young brave who had been killed by their hereditary foes, the Chippeways or Ojibways. The wailing of the mourners could be heard for miles, and I shall never forget the weird sound.

Some six miles north of the fort are the Falls of St. Anthony, and near by is the beautiful cascade, Minnehaha, or Laughing Waters. The former we saw in their primitive state, where now are the vast flouring mills, and other manufactories that are the glory and the foundation of the growth and prosperity of the city of Minneapolis of one hundred and fifty thousand people. The silence of death then reigned where now is heard the roar and excitement of business. St. Paul, the twin sister of Minneapolis, and of equal size, about six miles down the river on the opposite bank, was then only a fur-trading post. Off to the north and west of the Falls was a vast expanse of unbroken prairie, over which roamed the Indians, but which is now covered with towns and cities, and traversed by railroads in every direction. I wondered when, if ever, the region would be occupied by civilized men. How wonderful the change a few short years have wrought!

Dubuque, at this time, was a town of some fifteen hundred inhabitants, drawn there by the attractions of the lead mines, and much resembling the early gold-mining towns of California. The following extracts from an historical sermon that I preached on the fourth anniversary of my settlement there, will show the condition of my field of pastoral labor a little before I entered upon it:

In such a population there was none of the religious element, but, on the contrary, there was a total destitution of the fear of God, and, I had almost said, of regard for man. There was, of course, no recognition of the Sabbath, and no public worship, while vices of almost every kind were practised. A gentleman informs me that, wishing to procure a Bible, he searched the place in vain to find one, and actually was obliged to go to Galena to procure one.

After a time, three or four religious families came,

a prayer-meeting was established, and a Methodist circuit preacher began holding services once in four weeks, and Rev. A. Kent of Galena preached occasionally. Some idea of the state of morals in these early days may be formed from the following facts:

An editorial in the *Visitor*, printed here, said: "A minister is wanted here who can reason, preach, sing, and enforce the fourth commandment."

A correspondent of the *New York Journal of Commerce* wrote from here: "The principal amusement of the people seems to be playing cards, Sunday and all. The law they carry in their pockets, and are ready to read a chapter on the slightest occasion."

The Roman Catholics early made this an important point, and erected a church building in 1836. In 1838 a bishopric was established, and a bishop stationed here. This has since developed into an important archbishopric.

CHAPTER IX

Such was the place and such were the people where I began the chief work of my life, in March, 1842, and for which Divine Providence had been mysteriously preparing me in my previous course. It has always seemed to me wonderful how all things worked together for that result.

In the winter of 1835, a Presbyterian missionary had held services in the place. A Presbyterian church was formed which subsequently became Congregational, but it had never had a settled pastor. I found there a little band of nineteen male and female members, occupying an unfinished stone building, unplastered within, and furnished only with unpainted pine pulpit and seats, while the prayer-meetings were held in the basement, likewise unfinished, and lighted only at night by the candles which the members brought.

It was gloomy and unattractive in the extreme.

I had made considerable progress in theological study, and was pretty familiar, as I have said, with general literature. I was still young, thirty-four years of age, of sanguine spirit, in good health, and I entered upon my first pastorate there with immense enthusiasm. My first sermon was on the text, " My yoke is easy, and my burden is light," and it evidently made a favorable impression. I have the manuscript now, yellow with age and faded in the ink, and it is a fair sample of the spirit of all my subsequent discourses. The following July after my call, I attended the annual meeting of the Iowa Congregational Association at Davenport, and was duly ordained, Father Asa Turner preaching the sermon. In the following spring, the Mineral Point Congregational and Presbyterian Convention of Wisconsin, with which my church was then connected, met in Dubuque, and I was installed as pastor, Rev. S. Peet preaching the sermon.

As I have before said, my wife and second son had died some time before, and I was left with only my eldest son, a lad of some

THE OLD STONE CHURCH.

twelve years. Feeling the need of a helper in my new field, on the 18th of October, 1842, I was married to Miss Ann L. Clark of Platteville, Wisconsin, sister of the doctor who had been my family physician, and with whom I took the journey which resulted finally in my settlement in Dubuque. I agree with President Sturtevant who, referring to his second marriage in his interesting autobiography, says,—

I did not then, nor do I less now, subscribe to the doctrine, that a man painfully bereaved by the loss of his wife at the age of thirty-four, best honors the memory of the departed by remaining unmarried. The sweet remembrance of conjugal happiness is not a preparation for a life of loneliness.

I think I was most providentially directed in the choice of my new companion, as fifty-two years of experience in our after united life have abundantly proved. My wife was the daughter of a noble Christian mother, whose training of her children was remarkable, all of whom have demonstrated her wisdom and her holy influence. My wife proved to be a helpmeet indeed to me in all my subsequent career, sharing with me most bravely and cheerfully the toils and self-denial of my early ministry, and ever proving a safe counselor and coöperator with me in all my labors. But I will not dwell on this point, as I shall have occasion to say more when I record her lamented death, long years afterwards.

Having thus become settled in my new field of labor, I entered upon my work, I repeat, with immense enthusiasm. I soon accumulated a considerable library, and began in earnest the study of my Greek Testament and works on theology and homiletics. I had pretty well mastered Dwight's theology, and had also Knapp's excellent treatise, with those of Edwards, Emmons, Hopkins, and other New England writers, and I kept myself familiar with the current theological literature of the day. I rigidly set apart my forenoons for study, and never thus employed my evenings when I could avoid it, or denied myself needed sleep.

I resolved from the first never to enter my pulpit without a thorough preparation, when I could possibly avoid it. I would not indulge myself in the use of mere religious harangues or hortatory appeals, nor impose them upon my congregation. I carefully wrote out my sermons, and sought to make them practical and instructive, and always thoroughly logical. And in this last respect

I was greatly indebted to old Dr. Nathaniel Emmons, of whom it was said, that, grant him his premises and you could not possibly escape his conclusions. I did not, however, adopt all his peculiar points in theology.

I was early impressed with a sense of my responsibility in the position in which I had been so unexpectedly placed by Divine Providence. I used often, in leisure hours, to climb the high bluff back of the town, and, looking down on the mighty Mississippi flowing past with its lines of great steamers and upon the young city at my feet, and thinking of the thousands that would ere long walk its streets and of the vast region around as yet unsettled, but soon to teem with inhabitants that might be affected by my labors and feel the influence of an active and enterprising church that, by the blessing of God, I might be instrumental in building up, I was stimulated anew to consecrate my best abillities to the work set before me. I saw myself placed where I was called to do my utmost in shaping the character of a future large city, and to aid others in molding that of a mighty state, and I was almost overwhelmed with the thought.

The church, as I have said, was originally formed on the Presbyterian model, and its modest and unfinished house of worship was heavily mortgaged. It was impossible for the members to redeem it, so that it was about to be sold, and I could see no relief, but by an appeal for help to friends in New England. But those on whom I thought I could depend for help were Congregationalists, and would not feel, I thought, any special interest in the case. But just then an event occurred which solved the difficulty. There was but one ruling elder, and he had become very unpopular by reason of his dictatorial spirit. He sought to be emphatically a *ruling* elder, and he it was who had involved the church in debt. There was then a young man in the church who afterwards entered the ministry, and went as a home missionary to California, and later became the very efficient superintendent of the missions of the American Home Missionary Society in that state. Seeing no way of relieving the church from its embarrassment under the *ruling* elder, who could not be deposed, and who refused to resign, the young man referred to made a motion at a business meeting that *all* the members of the church should be elected ruling elders! This was carried, and presto, the body was transformed into a Congregational church. It soon after became such formally and in fact.

The way was now open for an appeal for pecuniary aid to Congregational friends in New England, and I was commissioned to visit that region, and to endeavor to secure the help needed to liquidate the mortgage on the church building. I undertook the task, and was kindly and cordially received in various places which I visited, and I returned home with six hundred dollars. Among the places visited was Bath, Maine, where I met Mr. George F. Magoun, who had just finished his collegiate course at Bowdoin, and his theological studies at Andover and Yale. He was very desirous of visiting the West, and solicited the privilege of accompanying me on my return home. He did so, and for a short time was my guest at Dubuque, and soon after became the principal of the academy at Platteville, Wisconsin. Subsequently, he was ordained as a minister, and at length became for several years the very efficient and successful president of Iowa college.   I little thought at the time, that I was introducing to his life-work in my state the afterwards distinguished head of its leading college.

Our journey was by way of the Ohio river, stopping a short time at Cincinnati. There we took a steamer for St. Louis, the captain of which assured us that we should reach our destination before Sunday.   But on Saturday it became apparent that we should not do so, and we told the captain to land us at some town that night, as we had scruples about traveling on Sunday.   But he seriously objected, and offered to allow us to hold public worship on the boat. We persisted, however, and were finally landed at a little town on the Kentucky side of the river, where we spent Sunday, and attended worship in a Presbyterian church.   On Monday morning, very early, another boat bound for St. Louis appeared, which we boarded, and on arriving at our port, we found the passengers we had left on Saturday evening had but just arrived there.   So we kept the Sabbath and lost no time.

CHAPTER X

BUILDING A NEW HOUSE OF WORSHIP—COM-
ING OF THE IOWA BAND—FOUNDING OF
IOWA COLLEGE—SOME WISCONSIN NEIGH-
BORS

On my return from New England, the
church made an effort with the party in
St. Louis that held the claim, to compro-
mise the debt on the house of worship, with
the aid of the money I had collected, but
without success, and we were obliged to
abandon the building, and to endeavor to
erect another. We found the citizens ready
to coöperate with us, and we at once set
about the work, holding services in the
meantime in the court-house, and in the
Baptist church, whose pulpit was vacant. I
visited Galena and secured from the owner
the offer of two very eligible lots on Main
street, one, the corner, for $350, and the
adjoining one for $300. I was in favor of
taking both, but the trustees of our newly
incorporated Congregational society did not
share my faith in the future of the city, or

feel that we were warranted in investing so large a sum in a site, and they decided to take the inner and cheaper lot. Some years afterward, when we erected the present large and beautiful structure, that original lot and building were sold for $20,000. Had we taken the two lots, as I desired, we should have been "pound wise" instead of "penny foolish."

A subscription was raised, by which, with the money I had collected in New England, we soon completed a neat and convenient building, which we occupied for several years, and which became the scene of several very precious revival seasons, to which I shall refer later. Fortunately, there had come into the church an experienced carpenter and builder, who drew the plan and superintended the erection of a building with a Grecian Ionic front, which was much admired at that early period in the history of the city.

In 1843, the year after my settlement, there came a notable addition to the ranks of the Congregational ministry. There were then but seven ordained ministers of the order in the territory, whom Dr. Roy, in Dunning's "History of Congregationalism,"

THE SECOND HOUSE.

calls "the sacred seven." They were Father Asa Turner, Julius A. Reed, Reuben Gaylord, Charles Burnham, Oliver Emerson, and myself, with Allen B. Hitchcock, who had recently come to Davenport from Yale seminary. This new addition to our strength consisted of the famous Iowa Band commissioned by the American Home Missionary society, and was composed of eleven young men from Andover Theological seminary. Part of them had been ordained, and the others were thus set apart for their work at Denmark, where Father Turner had established the first Congregational church in the territory.

One of their number was a humorist and fond of jokes, and while crossing the Mississippi, a high wind had nearly capsized their boat. On landing, he exclaimed, "Brethren, what a sensation would have been experienced at the East if we had all gone to the bottom!" Again, at the ordination, the duty of giving the usual charge was assigned to a young man of the council who was the least qualified for the service and who was not particularly impressive. Alluding to this after the adjournment, the facetious brother exclaimed to his associates, " What an idea, to set a man to charge us who was not half charged himself! "

To these new-comers were assigned stations in various parts of the territory from the Missouri line to the county north of Dubuque. They soon established churches, local associations were formed, and they entered enthusiastically into the work of evangelizing the territory. In this their services proved highly important and valuable, and to them is due much of the credit of making Iowa what it has become, one of the noblest states of the Middle West. It has indeed been called " the Massachusetts of the West." Its immigrants have been more largely of the better class than those of any of its sister states, and it has the lowest degree of illiteracy of any of them.

It had always been the purpose of the pioneer Congregational ministers to found a Christian college at an early date, and some steps had been taken in that direction. This new band entered fully into the design, and it was ultimately carried into execution; and from a first graduation class of two, it has since sent out hundreds, and has taken rank among the best institutions of the kind in the West. It is an interesting fact, worthy of record here, that among the very first contributions towards its endowment was a pledge of $10 each from the wives of the ministers and home missionaries, made at a meeting of the General Association at Dubuque!

Several of the members of the band were stationed near Dubuque, and it was my privilege often to entertain them at my house, and to assist them in their work. My house was always open to their visits, and I visited them, and aided them in revival meetings. My church, being the oldest and largest in the northern section of the territory, became, of course, a centre of influence. I was one of the original members of the Dubuque Association. I found in these young men very congenial fellow-laborers, where I had stood alone, with no ministerial neighbor north or west of me, the nearest Congregational minister in Iowa being an itinerant at some distance south.

I was, however, highly favored in being early associated with a choice band of ministers of a congenial spirit with my own, on the opposite side of the Mississippi, in the southwest corner of Wisconsin. For a time. indeed, I was called to labor much in that section, holding revival meetings, my church generously allowing me to do so. I think there never was a more devoted body of ministers than were these. They were Rev. J. D. Stevens, who had been a missionary of the American Board among the Sioux Indians; Rev. John Lewis, of sainted memory, whose wife was a daughter of the well-known Harlan Page, the devoted layman of New York; Zachary Eddy, afterwards an eloquent pastor in Brooklyn, New York, Detroit, Michigan, and Atlanta, Georgia; D. B. Bradford, C. Warner, and George F. Magoun, afterwards the distinguished president of Iowa College; and S. W. Eaton, father of the president of Beloit College. All these have passed on to their reward except the last-named, who, with his wife, has lately celebrated their golden wedding at Roscoe, Illinois.

CHAPTER XI

EARLY LABORS IN DUBUQUE—A HISTORICAL
DISCOURSE—PROGRESS OF CHURCH AND
CITY

The first four years of my new pastorate were
years of severe labor and no little self-denial.
The church was small and poor, and my salary, which, as I have said, was fixed at $600,
was not always paid in full, though eked out
for a little time by an appropriation from the
missionary society in New York. But with
the help of my devoted wife, and the strictest
economy, we managed to live and keep out
of debt. My labors were blessed, there was
a constantly growing congregation, and I
found my influence in the community increasing. We completed our new house of worship
without a debt, and at the dedication I
preached a historical sermon, which was
printed by request of some leading citizens,
including several who did not belong to my
congregation, and from which I give some
extracts. It was delivered in April, 1846,
four years after my settlement.

The text was, Acts 28 : 15, " He thanked God, and took courage."

A great change has taken place in the general aspect of what has now become a city, and Episcopal and Baptist churches have been added to our own, and the Methodist and Roman Catholic. Valuable additions have been made to our population, and a United States land office, and surveyor general's office have been established here, which have given additional importance to the place.

When I began my labors, the church was in a state of great depression, encumbered by a heavy debt, and with no prospect of its liquidation. There were but nineteen resident members, and not more than five or six were present at the prayer-meeting. But soon a good congregation began attending public worship, and from time to time there were conversions and additions to the church membership. In the course of the first winter, 1842–'43, I was called to assist pastors in revivals in the neighboring state of Wisconsin, and towards spring there were encouraging signs of increasing religious interest in our church, but the members had had no experience in revivals.

I therefore prepared and delivered a series of discourses on the subject, setting forth encouragements and duties, and it was not long before the way opened for a series of daily meetings, which continued about ten days, and there was a general work of grace, whose effects were very salutary, and there was a considerable addition to the church, as there has been every year since, until now. At the end of four years, there is a membership of fifty-three, only eleven of whom were members when I came. It was a dark and gloomy day when we abandoned our house of worship at the beginning of this period, and the world regarded our case as hopeless; but God rewarded our faith, and behold what he hath wrought! Struggling as we did for our very existence, we yet have contributed for the general cause of home and foreign missions, and we have mingled our prayer, " Thy kingdom come," with that of Christians the world over. We have never known dissension among us, but have been of one heart and mind, and we now enter upon a new era with more to encourage us than at any previous period of our history.

In concluding this discourse, I said:

What a moral change has been wrought in this place, already, by the gospel! It is still fresh in the memory of many, when there was scarcely more of a Sabbath here than when the smoke of the Indian wigwam rose from the valley, and the savage yell of the native broke the stillness of the air. But now the quietude that reigns on the Lord's day bespeaks another influence in the community, and our town would not unfavorably compare with the majority of others of equal population in most parts of the land. One gentleman informs me that he remembers when, a few years ago, he saw on a single Sunday in our streets horse-racing, foot-racing, card-playing, drinking of intoxicating liquors, fighting, wrestling, and the transaction of business, while few were bending their steps to hear the word of God. But now how different, when several places of worship are open and filled with attentive hearers! What would this place have been without a ministry and church? How much we have, then, to encourage us to labor on in the work of evangelization here! I pledge myself and you of this church, to hearty coöperation with Christians of all denominations, in this glorious and blessed work. Our responsibilities are great, for we are laying foundations for many generations; thousands here, and tens of thousands in the surrounding country, are to be affected by our acts—nay, to a great extent, the whole future population of this great state of Iowa will feel our influence. Think of the thousands that will people these streets, and swarm over these prairies, and you cannot fail to be impressed with the importance of our work. Let Christians of all denominations lay aside all petty jealousies, and all rivalry except in doing good, and let them unite in energetic and harmonious action and fervent prayer for the triumph of the gospel here, and we shall see still greater evidence than we have witnessed, of its power to promote peace, harmony, morality, and happiness.

It is with sincere gratitude that I here record the goodness of God in favoring the church, as I have said, with numerous revivals of religion. We saw some dark days, and struggled through many difficulties and obstacles, but we never despaired, and we were rewarded for our faith. The year following the delivery of the historical discourse from which I have quoted, occurred the fourth season of refreshing from on high. It was remarkable in some respects, and wrought such a change in the strength of the church and in the moral aspect of the community as can hardly now be realized. It more than trebled the membership of the church, and quadrupled its efficiency. It continued six weeks, and in the absence of ministerial help I was compelled to preach every evening, preparing new sermons and attending prayer and inquiry meetings in addition, " the Lord adding to us daily such as should be saved."

One remarkable feature of this work was that it included in its subjects a large number of leading members of society here. Among these was the United States district judge and his wife, several prominent lawyers, physicians, merchants, and others. Our house of worship became too small and its dimensions were soon doubled, and a large and convenient addition was made in the rear for prayer-meetings and the Sabbath-school. This work was a severe tax upon the physical, mental, and spiritual energies of the pastor, but God fulfilled his promise, "As thy days, so shall thy strength be." I found that then I was enabled to preach the best sermons of my life, and sermons which have proved effective in many such seasons since.

During the period of my first pastorate of eleven years, the territory of Iowa, with a population of only 50,000, had been erected into a state, bounded on the east by the Mississippi river, on the west by the mighty Missouri, and extending from the north line of the state of Missouri to the south line of the new territory of Minnesota, and had large accessions to its inhabitants of an exceptionally valuable character. The place, which on my arrival was only a mining village of fifteen hundred people, with but one or two brick buildings, had developed into a considerable city, with fine residences, and large blocks for business purposes, and was showing signs of becoming, as it has since become, an important centre of business for a large region west and north, while the church grew from nineteen members to be the second in numbers in the state.

For some years in my early ministry at Dubuque I maintained an extensive correspondence with our Eastern religious newspapers, the New York *Observer*, the Boston *Recorder*, and afterwards the Boston *Congregationalist*. I was the regular Western correspondent of the New York *Independent* in its early years, when it was edited by Rev. Drs. J. P. Thompson, R. S. Storrs, and Leonard Bacon, with Joshua Leavitt as office editor. I early advocated the plan of aiding new churches in erecting houses of worship, then quite an unpopular idea, and I specially contended for the right of planting Congregational churches in the West, which was opposed violently by leading Presbyterians. A little before this, there were the beginnings of what proved to be a mighty contest for this right in Illinois and in Iowa, which finally culminated in the Albany convention, to be described further on, which repudiated the famous plan of union between Congregationalists and Presbyterians, so disastrous to the interests of the former. Rev. Dr. Pond, now of San Francisco, was then a theological student at Bangor, Maine, and he has since told me that my writings on this subject deeply moved his spirit and inspired him with a strong desire to buckle on his armor and plunge into the fray.

CHAPTER XII

I was converted in a revival of religion, and I have ever since been a firm believer in the value and importance of such seasons. I had labored and prayed from the beginning of my pastorate for such blessings, and I was not disappointed. I early adopted the practice of old Dr. Beecher, who said, "When circumstances favored, I engaged in efforts for a revival, and I was never disappointed in the result." I believe that those pastors who expect and plan and labor and pray for such refreshings are favored with them, while those who do not do so rarely enjoy them. I think the great majority of those who united with my church during my entire ministry were converted in such seasons, and my testimony is, that they were generally among the most spiritual and steadfast of the members. The *proportion* of those who afterwards fell away was, I am sure, not greater than, if as great as, that of those who became members under the ordinary manner of grace. My experience also was, that many who were brought into the church in revivals were from outside of my regular congregation. Such works of grace extend their influence beyond the bounds of the regular congregation, and this is one of the reasons why they are so desirable in a community. If pastors only gather into their churches the members of the Sabbath-school, and those of their regular congregations, what is to become of what are called "outsiders"?

I know it is said that "a church ought to be always in a revived state." But what ought to be is not the fact, ordinarily, and, if so, what is to be done but to pray and labor for a revival? The first Christian church was born in a revival at Pentecost, and the great revivals that have since blessed the world have been, seemingly, the salvation of the church. Those in this country, at the beginning of this century, were the means of turning back the tide of French infidelity that threatened to sweep over our land. In one such season in my own church a man was converted who was not then a member of my congregation, and he afterwards paid $5,000, and saved the house of worship from sale for debt.

I thank God for revivals, and I have labored in many, not only in my own parish but with my brethren in other places, in Iowa, Wisconsin and Illinois, and later in New York state.

I remember one such season of great power in the First Presbyterian Church in the city of Galena, of which Rev. A. Kent was pastor. I preached daily for several weeks, and among the converts were a large number of the heads of some of the most prominent families in the city, and among the results was the formation of two additional Presbyterian churches. In Grant county, Wisconsin, where was that choice band of ministers to which I have before referred, and with whom I was associated, I conducted revival services in all their churches, as well as in other places where there was no church, and where churches were formed as the result. For several winters much of my time was thus employed, my church cheerfully allowing me the time and opportunity. I recall more than twenty places where I thus labored—Prairie du Chien, Potosi, Lancaster, Blake's Prairie,

Elk Grove, Platteville, Hazel Green, Mineral Point (Dr. Eddy's church), Shullsburgh, Fairplay, all in Wisconsin, Galena and Nora, in Illinois, and besides Dubuque, in Iowa, Durango, Andrew, Belleview, Anamosa, Maquoketa, Lyons, Cascade, Iowa City, Garnavillo, Colesburgh and others. In one case, for want of a suitable building, a successful meeting was held in a barn, and it resulted in the erection of a house of worship; and in another case, the meetings were in a bowling alley, generously offered by the proprietor. The billiard table was the desk, the balls and pins piled in the corner, and the liquor saloon in the opposite end separated by a partition, the sound of the toddy stick mingling with the preacher's voice! But God blessed the work, and souls were saved.

Some years later I published a series of articles in a local religious paper in Dubuque, the *Newsletter*, describing some of those scenes, and they were afterwards issued in a small book by Henry Hoyt, Sunday-school bookseller in Cornhill, Boston, and many editions were sold.

It is worthy of record here, also, that at the semi-centennial celebration of the Dubuque church, it was estimated that twelve young men of that church under my ministry had become preachers of the gospel.   Among them was Rev. Dr. J. H. Warren, for many years the superintendent of Home Missions in California, Rev. Albert Bale, long a successful pastor at Melrose, near Boston, and Reverends John H. and William Windsor, sons of an English lay preacher who had come to reside in Dubuque, and was carrying on, for a time, a vegetable garden in the suburbs.   His two sons were converted under my ministry, and joined my church.

One day the eldest came to my house on an errand, and on his departure I followed him to the gate, and said, " John, don't you think you ought to be a minister?"   It seemed to strike him like a bolt of electricity, and it awakened a thought that had never dawned upon him before.   Soon after that, I was at the father's place and saw the other son hoeing in the melon patch, and I accosted him in the same manner, and with the same result. But they could see no way of preparation, for want of pecuniary means.

But, fortunately, I had a wealthy friend in New London, Connecticut, who was in the habit of aiding promising young men in gaining an education for the ministry, and I applied to him for help in the case of these two individuals. He at once responded favorably, and placed them on his list of candidates, and ultimately saw them through college and the theological seminary. They were the first two graduates of Iowa college, and have since proved eminently successful and useful Congregational ministers. I have always regarded my agency in thus bringing forth for this service these two and other young men as one of the opportunities of doing good for which I am grateful to Providence, and I cannot but think that every pastor should make this one leading object in his work for Christ.

In 1851 I was elected a corporate member of the American Board of Commissioners for Foreign Missions, and at the time of this writing (1897) I am one of the three oldest surviving members of the Board. I have always, from the beginning of my Christian life, felt a deep interest in the foreign as well as home missionary work. One of my earliest efforts in doing good, after my conversion, was in taking a leading part in sustaining the monthly concert of prayer in the church in my native place, and one of the first things I did after entering on my first pastorate was to establish such a concert for my church, a *home* missionary church though it was.

During my early pastorate at Dubuque I attended several important conventions. The first was a gathering of the friends of education in Wisconsin and northern Illinois, to consider the establishment of a college at Beloit. In the early days of my ministry at Dubuque, I was, as I have said, intimately associated with brethren in Wisconsin. Indeed, my church at first was connected with the Mineral Point, Wisconsin, convention, just across the Mississippi, and I was installed by that body in my pastorate, hence my attendance at the educational convention referred to at Beloit. It was there decided to found a college on the New England model, at Beloit, on the immediate border of Illinois, and at the same time to establish a female seminary (since called a college) of high grade at Rockford near by, and just south of the line between the two states, in the expectation that both states would share the benefits of both institutions. The plan was carried out successfully, and both have taken the first rank among such institutions.

CHAPTER XIII

I come now to speak of what may justly be
called a memorable epoch in the history of
Congregationalism in the United States, when
the denomination and its system may be said
to have become national instead of provincial.
Hitherto it had been mainly confined to New
England. The famous Plan of Union between Congregationalists and Presbyterians
of 1801 had practically operated to absorb
Congregational ministers and members into
the Presbyterian body, until it had come to be
claimed that the Presbyterians had—to use a
land-office term—" preëmpted " the West, and
that to establish a Congregational church
there was to trespass on another's claim.
Even old Dr. Woods of Andover, and some
other leading men, advised ministers and
members of churches going West to fall into
the Presbyterian ranks. As a result, it is
estimated that two thousand churches that
should naturally have been Congregational

actually became Presbyterian, including quite a number that originally were formed Congregationally, but were so transformed.

After a time, the rivalry between the Old School and New School parties in the Presbyterian body had become very intense, and President Sturtevant, in his "Autobiography," says :

No one unfamiliar with the struggle can form any conception of the intense hostility of the New School party towards the spread of Congregationalism west of the Hudson. They regarded New England immigration as the chief means by which their numbers and influence were to be augmented, and considered the organization of Congregational churches a violation of good faith, claiming that the Plan of Union was a solemn league and covenant whereby New England was permanently guaranteed to Congregationalism, and the whole region West, "even to the going down of the sun," consecrated to Presbyterianism !

As the editor of the *Advance* puts it,—

The Plan of Union was the first part of the "Courtship of Miles Standish" over again. The Congregational Priscilla, having gone west of the Hudson, is urged to unite her fortunes with that of Miles Standish Presbyterian, and while it was going on she spun and wove for the second-hand suitor, and assisted in establishing a large number of Presbyterian households ; but at the last she said, "Why do n't you speak for yourself, John

Alden?' and he did, with the result that Congregationalism marched westward with the star of empire, and became a notable factor in American ecclesiastical development. An intelligent lady once remarked that Congregationalism took its rise in New England and flowed west
and emptied into Presbyterianism."

Rev. Dr. Roy writes in "Dunning's History of Congregationalism":

Rev. A. T. Norton, in his "History of Presbyterianism in Illinois," says, that after investigation it was his
full belief that one half its members have been and are
New Englanders. And while the two denominations
were united in the American Home Missionary Society,
it was ascertained that while two thirds of the aided
churches were Presbyterian, two thirds of the money
came from Congregational sources. Milk from Congregational cows churned into Presbyterian butter."

The resultant of the Plan of Union was not arrested
until a Congregational convention was held in 1846, in
Michigan City, Indiana, which protested against this denominational abnegation, and the Albany convention
afterwards repudiated the entangling alliance.

Previously to this, there had begun some
movements for the founding of Congregational
churches ; the Michigan City convention, 1846,
gave it a new impulse, and there was developed an excitement in the West that cannot
be realized now by any who were not then on
the stage of active life, nor the violence of

the contention for, and the opposition to, the right of Congregationalists to propagate their system. Illinois was at first the chief storm centre.

In and around Jacksonville, Illinois, there were a number of graduates of Yale Theological Seminary, and some of them took decided ground in favor of organizing Congregational churches. Among these was Rev. Asa Turner, familiarly called afterwards in Iowa, "Father Turner," who organized two such churches in Illinois, at Quincy and Mendon, and was denounced for doing so. Even Dr. Lyman Beecher, then president of Lane Theological Seminary, wrote him, reprimanding him for his course, and even threatening him, if he persisted in it, with being "put down." But he was not appalled, and soon after removed to Iowa, where he established the first church of the order and laid the first stone in the noble edifice of Congregationalism in that state.

When Rev. J. M. Sturtevant, the first professor in Illinois College, who was then a member of a presbytery, organized the Congregational church in Jacksonville, he was even threatened with being disciplined by his associates of that body for the act. He tells us, in his interesting "Autobiography," that,—

At that time, the church at Jacksonville had no nearer [Congregational] neighbors than Princeton, Mendon, Quincy, and Naperville, where they had all been established, except the first, within a year. Nor had we any reason to expect that others would soon be formed. These churches were the first evidence of open revolt against the operation of the Plan of Union. Most of the Congregational churches in New Jersey, northeastern Pennsylvania, northern Ohio, and Long Island [and in the interior of New York state], were under the guardianship of the General Assembly, and were rapidly becoming absorbed in the Presbyterian body. Had not some stand been made against this movement, Congregationalism would soon have become extinct in all parts of the United States except New England. . . . But now, within fifty years, a greater number of Congregational churches have been established in the West and South than ever existed in New England.

Dr. Sturtevant tells us that after his agency in the organization of the church in Jacksonville, he visited New York and called on Dr. Peters, then secretary of the Home Missionary Society, and was called to account by him for his course, and he adds that this was by no means the only incident in which he found that his conduct in the case referred to was disapproved by eminent friends of his.

7

Dr. Joel Hawes of Hartford, however, greatly confirmed him in his determination "to adhere to the broad principles of Congregationalism." But he says, "Many-tongued rumor in the West spread abroad the insinuation that my thinking was wild, erratic, and dangerous."

"During all his residence in the West," says Dr. Sturtevant, "Dr. Lyman Beecher favored Presbyterianism. Several times on meeting him after a long separation, almost his first question would be, 'How are you getting on with those rabid Congregationalists in Illinois?' My ready reply was, 'We should get along well enough if it were not for the rabid Presbyterians.' This was received with good nature. After he returned to the East, he had little difficulty in finding out where he belonged. His great heart was with the freedom of Congregationalism."

Other churches, after those referred to, began to be formed in Illinois, Michigan, Wisconsin, and Iowa, and at length there followed, not long after, the movement in Chicago,—which will be described later—which, with the actions of the Albany convention and the Boston council, settled the question of the right and duty of Congregationalists to extend their system in any part of the land, and, I may add, in any part of the world where Providence should open the way.

It had been more than two hundred years since the last great representative gathering of Congregationalists had met, viz., the Cambridge Synod, when the General Association of New York issued an invitation for a general convention to meet in Albany to consider the interests of the denomination. This was at once responded to by the churches, and on the 5th of October, 1852, the convention, consisting of four hundred and sixty-three members, assembled at the appointed place. I was a delegate, with several others, from Iowa. Rev. W. T. Dwight, D. D., a son of the first President Dwight of Yale College, who had been originally a lawyer, presided with great dignity and efficiency. Rev. Dr. Noah Porter of Connecticut, and Rev. Asa Turner of Iowa, were assistants. I acted as one of the secretaries, with Rev. R. S. Storrs and L. S. Hobart.

Very injurious and unfounded reports had been industriously circulated by the opponents of Congregationalism in the West, to the effect that great unsoundness in the faith and looseness of discipline prevailed among the Congregationalists, and that the polity was not adapted to the West, where a stronger and more stringent one was needed. These reports had been credited to some extent in New England, and had excited prejudice and led some to doubt the propriety of seeking to extend the Congregational system in that section of the land.

This convention gave to the Western men the opportunity to vindicate themselves, and the work was very effectively done, so that entire harmony prevailed in all the sessions. The plan of union was abrogated by a unanimous vote, and other action was taken which may be regarded as a very important step in introducing the new era in the history of the denomination. This was followed by another, later, the Boston Council, which was the culmination of the measures which delivered the denomination from all the obstacles that had hitherto obstructed its expansion. But it was not without a severe struggle that peace was at last won by the perseverance of the Congregational saints.

At the convention in Albany, another step was taken that has resulted in great advantage to the Congregational denomination in its home missionary work. The Iowa brethren had for some time been urging the importance of aiding new churches in the West in erecting houses of worship, but with little success. When appeals were made for help in this direction to Eastern men, the response came back, "We will aid in supplying ministers, but you must build your own churches." And even some of the religious papers at the East declined to publish communications on the subject. A few private individuals had responded, however, with donations to private appeals, and I had the pleasure of administering some of these donations.

This subject was one of the topics of discussion at the convention. It was then that Mr. Bowen, of the firm of Bowen & McNamee, merchants of New York city, made the offer of $10,000 towards a fund of $50,000 for this purpose, provided the balance was raised by the churches. This was referred to a committee, of which I was one. The other members hesitated, being elderly and conservative in their views, and Mr. Bowen afterwards published the fact that I was the only member who, with him, heartily advocated and approved the measure. We at length succeeded, however, in securing a report from the committee, recommending a general and simultaneous collection by the churches, and it was adopted by the body, and as the result over $67,000 were raised. This was the beginning of a movement which resulted in the formation of the Congregational Church Building Society, which, under the efficient management of Secretary L. H. Cobb, D. D., has proved a most efficient auxiliary to the Home Missionary Society in the prosecution of its great work. It has had one legacy of about $250,000.

And here I may as well refer to another general representative gathering of Congregationalists, already spoken of, of which I was a member, although it was not held until a few years later, namely, the important *Boston Council*, memorable in the annals of the denomination. It was held in the historic Old South Church in that city, June 14, 1865, and Hon. William A. Buckingham, governor of Connecticut, presided, assisted by Hon. Charles G. Hammond of Chicago and Rev. Dr. J. P. Thompson of New York city.

Out of this has grown the National Congregational Council, which meets triennially, of which I have several times been a member. It has no controlling or legislative power over the churches, but meets to consider the various interests of the denomination, and to discuss and to advise in regard to ways of carrying on its work.

Says Dr. Dunning in his " History of Congregationalism":

The work and necessities of the various denominational societies were considered at this Boston Council, and generous sympathy was expressed for the other undenominational associations. The Bible, Sunday-school, Education and Tract Societies, and ministerial relief, systematic beneficence, church building, and home and foreign missions received attention.

But the subject of most absorbing interest was the duty of caring for the three or four millions of slaves just emancipated and thrown upon their own resources. As a beginning the Council advised the raising of seven hundred and fifty thousand dollars for the work, and the churches responded nobly.

The enthusiasm manifested in the body was great, and entire harmony prevailed, all jealousies and differences of diferent " schools " were laid aside, and there was a perfect exhibition of the unity of the Spirit in the bonds of love.

The American Missionary Association at New York, supported mainly by Congregationalists, took up the work of evangelizing and educating this great body of enfranchised slaves, now amounting to some seven millions, and has prosecuted it with great zeal and success; and that is the Association for which I undertook a mission for raising funds for this object, to which I shall refer further on.

The council also recommended a platform of church polity and a declaration of faith. The latter was adopted under peculiar circumstances of great interest. "Then came into being," says Professor Walker, "the only declaration of faith which a body representative of American Congregationalism, as a whole, had approved since 1648," and none has been set forth since.

The council had adjourned to Plymouth, where the Pilgrims landed and established the first church. In the elevated burying-ground where they were interred, the declaration was read and solemnly adopted, all standing with uncovered heads, Rev. Dr. Ray Palmer, author of the hymn, "My Faith Looks Up to Thee," offering prayer, and the hymn and the doxology were sung. The document opens with these words: "Standing by the rock where the Pilgrims set foot on these shores, where they worshiped God, and among the graves of the early generations, we, the elders and messengers of the Congregational churches, acknowledging no rule of faith but the Word of God, do now declare our adherence to the faith and apostolic order of the primitive churches held by our fathers," etc. Then follows the statement of belief.

Rev. J. P. Gulliver, D. D., writing of this scene to the New York *Independent*, said:

It was a sublime moment! Nearly two hundred and fifty years had passed since the feeble Mayflower company had repeated in solemn covenant the articles of their despised faith on that spot. Now five hundred men, the representatives of five thousand churches, the representatives of ideas which have triumphed gloriously and finally over the land, the representatives of *Puritanism*, pure and simple, unchanged, unabashed, bold and intense as in the days of the Commonwealth, stood on the soil made firm by the heroic tread of these despised men, and exultingly declared, "This faith is our faith." These ideas have saved our country and are going forth, conquering and to conquer, over the world.

There were two delegates to the council from the Congregational Union of England and Wales, Rev. Drs. Vaughn and Raleigh. All the sessions were harmonious and deeply interesting, and Rev. Henry Ward Beecher, among others, made a most spirited address. This council, and the Albany convention already described, gave a new impulse to Congregationalism, and since then its spread over the continent to the Pacific ocean has been marvelous.

"It is due to the scope of history," says Dr. Dunning, referring to this period in his elaborate work, "Congregationalism in America," "to put on record the fact that the Congregational system, by its advanced ideas on the question of slavery, and its freedom from all organic connection with it, and from the ecclesiastical machinery of Presbyterianism, gained largely, not only by the turning back of Plan of Union churches, but in the organization of new churches—enough nearly to counterbalance the loss by the old-time coöperation."

In concluding the subject of this memorable epoch, which began a new era in the history of Congregationalism, it should be said that the early fathers of New England were undoubtedly sincere in their desire to avoid the multiplication of sects in the new states, and unwisely consented not to propagate their system, but, as President Sturtevant remarks, "They lost sight of the fundamentally antisectarian principles of their system. They should have remembered and enforced the broad Scriptural rule of Christian fellowship (which Congregationalism embodies) and held it sacred as the only solvent by which all sects can become one in Christ Jesus."

Had they done this, and manfully stood by and encouraged those who went forth from them in carrying the system wherever they went, which had made New England such a light in the world, the great schism of old and new schoolisms in the Presbyterian church would not have occurred, and New England would have been reproduced in many states of the West. It seems strange that up to the beginning of the revolt against the Plan of Union in the West, as President Sturtevant says, " The leading minds in the New England churches fully believed in that ' Plan,' and accepted the fruits which it was producing. They consented to the limitation of Congregationalism to New England, and surrendered with little regret the vast territory west and south of the Hudson to Presbyterianism."

Happily, as we have seen, the spell was finally broken, the eyes of Eastern men were opened, and the heroic men who contested the right of Congregationalism to plant itself anywhere and everywhere were at length sustained, and a peace was conquered that now prevails, the heretofore contending forces happily working harmoniously side by side in the great work of home evangelization.

CHAPTER XIV

In the preceding chapter I have anticipated
a little the chronological course of events, in
order to bring together the two great convoca-
tions, the Albany Convention and the Boston
Council, which had such a decisive influence
on the progress of Congregationalism. The
first of these great gatherings occurred in
1852, and the other in 1865.

As we have seen, the revolt against the disastrous Plan of Union had begun in Central
Illinois by the organization of several Congregational churches; the Michigan City vol-
unteer convention in 1846 had given it an
additional impulse, and in 1851 the first step
was taken in Chicago which gave new force
to the movement for the emancipation of Congregationalists from the entangling alliance
with Presbyterianism.

"It was not," says Dr. Roy, "until 1851

that Congregationalism found a foothold in Chicago, when forty-two of sixty-eight members of the Third Presbyterian church in that city, having been excluded from the church by the presbytery on account of their attitude on the slavery question, called a council, and were recognized as the First Congregational church of Chicago. Only four such churches could be found within a radius of forty miles. The next year Plymouth church, the second of the order, was formed." Now (1897) there are about seventy such within the city limits, more than in any other city in the world, and the Chicago association of churches is the largest such body known in any land, and there are more than three hundred such churches in the state. "The last half century," continues Dr. Roy, "is a distinct period in the history of the denomination. During that time it has awakened to a new self-consciousness, and has become national."

The formation of the First and Plymouth churches, followed by that of the New England, was not only the birth of Congregationalism in Chicago, but the beginning of a widespread development in the middle and north West; but there was a mighty struggle on the part of its friends to conquer a peace, and establish its right to be in the West.

About this time I was deeply afflicted by the death of my eldest son, a young man of nineteen years, a member of my church, who gave promise, had health permitted, of becoming a useful man. And so passed away the last of my first family, who are laid at rest, far apart, from Vermont to Iowa, while I look forward to repose in Stockton, California, beside my second wife.

And now (1853) occurred another of those marked interpositions of Providence in my affairs, of which I have so many to record, which again changed all my plans, and opened up to me what was, in some respects, an entirely new field of labor. When Plymouth Church, the second Congregational church in Chicago, was ready to dedicate its new house of worship, they cast about for some one to preach the sermon who was known as a pronounced and active advocate of the principles and rights of their denomination, and they called on me to perform the service. My letters in the *Independent* and my labors in Iowa had attracted the attention of those who were engaged in the new movement, and this, I suppose, led to

my selection to perform the required duty.
I accepted the invitation, and preached the
sermon, Rev. L. Smith Hobart, of Michigan,
making the dedicatory prayer. The next
morning after the service one of the daily
papers published the following report:

DEDICATION OF THE PLYMOUTH CONGREGATIONAL
CHURCH.

This church was dedicated on Sunday evening last.
The Rev. Mr. Holbrook of Dubuque preached in the
morning, and Rev. Mr. Hobart of Ann Arbor, in the
afternoon. At the afternoon service, W. H. Taylor, J. R.
Shedd, J. Johnson, and Mr. Broad were ordained as deacons. The charge was given by the Rev. Mr. Holbrook, and the consecrating prayer was made by Rev.
Mr. Hobart.

In the evening, the large house was crowded to its
utmost capacity. Rev. J. C. Holbrook preached the
dedication sermon. We could not be present ourselves,
but heard it spoken of as a very appropriate, able and
eloquent discourse. Rev. Mr. Hobart made the dedicatory prayer.

The church is sufficiently commodious to accommodate
a large congregation, and is in all respects worthy of the
Christian liberality of its founders.

The progress of this church is a fair example of the
way we do things in Chicago. It will be recollected that
it was organized with some fifty members, on the first day
of December last. The ground on which their building
now stands was then covered with a number of small

tenements. Within two months, these have all been removed, and a neat, commodious church edifice has been built and dedicated, and what is better, it is *paid for*. The pastor's salary has been increased and paid, and $200 have been given towards the Congregational fund, to build churches at the West. A number of persons are propounded for admission next Sabbath, and when admitted, there will be some eighty members connected with this new church. This certainly speaks volumes for the energy and Christian enterprise of those who have projected and carried out this new religious effort. It is just what we should expect of the sons and daughters of the Puritans.

We hope it will be remembered that there will be preaching in this church every afternoon at 3 o'clock, and every evening at 7 o'clock during the week. Rev. J. C. Holbrook of Dubuque and Rev. Mr. Hobart of Ann Arbor will assist the pastor in these protracted services.

While I was thus in Chicago, it was learned that the *Prairie Herald*, a so-called union religious weekly paper of that city, was for sale, and it was suggested that it should be purchased for a Congregational organ, and that I should become its editor. But I at first declined on the ground that I was unwilling to give up the pastoral work, to which I was much attached. To meet this objection, it was then proposed to form a *third* Congregational church, under my ministry, and that with this I should combine the editorship. This seemed to me a providential call to an enlarged field of usefulness, and I at once accepted it on condition that I should be released from my charge at Dubuque. I accordingly returned home and laid the matter before my church and asked them to call an ecclesiastical council for advice. To this they very reluctantly agreed, and a council was called, which, after considerable discussion, finally voted to recommend my dismission for the purpose named. I then removed my family to Chicago and entered upon my new work in 1853.

Several individuals united with me in the purchase of the paper, whose name was changed to *The Congregational Herald*, and it was placed under my control. At the same time, steps were taken for the organization of a new church, several prominent individuals agreeing to lead in the new enterprise. Meetings were at first held in the North Market hall, on the "north side," which I conducted, and in a short time a church organization was effected, and deacons and trustees were elected. Soon afterwards, a house of worship in that division of the city was erected, and the name, "New England Church," was adopted. We were fortunate in having for one of our leaders and deacons

8

a prominent citizen and railroad superintendent, and an ardent and widely-known Congregationalist, Col. C. G. Hammond. He was also one of those associated with me in the purchase of the paper, and afterwards one of the large contributors to the theological seminary established in the city. In our new church and congregation, also, there was a large body of young people of both sexes, who added much to the efficiency of the new enterprise. Deacon Philo Carpenter of the First Church, to whom the theological seminary owes so much for his pecuniary liberality, and Deacon Joseph Johnson of Plymouth Church were both very helpful to our new church. They were also contributors for the purchase of the paper. Rev. L. Smith Hobart, before referred to, and Rev. G. S. F. Savage aided much in launching the new church enterprise. Subsequently, E. W. Blatchford, vice-president of the American Board, and W. H. Bradley, Esq., clerk of the United States District Court, became members of the new church and added greatly to its strength and final success.

This period, as I have intimated, was one of great excitement and no little controversy, and the paper, of course, supported the claims of the Congregationalists. But it should be distinctly understood, that neither my brethren nor myself were engaged in opposing the legitimate efforts of Presbyterians to extend their system and multiply their churches, but we were simply contending for the right, which was disputed, of Congregationalists to do the same. We insisted that wherever there were those who preferred the Congregational polity, they should be allowed to adopt it and form churches of that order, without opposition and without reproach or _suspicion. We were then of the opinion expressed some years later by Rev. Dr. C. L. Goodell of St. Louis in an address before the Congregational Club of Chicago, that,

Congregationalism should no longer be regarded as local, but universal. As republicanism, which came in the compact in the *Mayflower*, went across the continent and spans a free people from sea to sea, so must the polity of the church do that sailed in the same ship. It has the same adaptations and fitnesses and desirability and strength. We have been too slow to grasp this fact. We have crept timidly where we should have marched forward in faith and courage, strong in the principle with which God armed us. * * * There has been a blind unbelief in the ability of Congregationalism to meet the wants of men. "There is no material here for Congregationalism" has been the cry of too many good men.

I declare to you, that wherever there is a soul to save there is material for Congregational work. Call it denominational zeal if you will; I call it devotion to the great truths on which we are founded."

The end for which we contended was finally secured, and peace and harmony were restored, and since then there has been a good degree of comity observed by both parties in their work of evangelization and "Ephraim no longer envies Judah, nor does Judah vex Ephraim." Each wishes for the prosperity of the other in its work for the common Master. There is something worse than war, a timid and cowardly submission to wrong, a yielding of principle for the sake of peace. "First pure, then peaceable."

In editing the new paper, I was aided to some extent by the other Congregational pastors in the city, but the whole management of the paper, financial and editorial, devolved on me, and I found the double duty of editor and pastor required the exercise of my utmost ability, both mental and physical. The paper gained a very considerable circulation in the West, and did much to stimulate the friends of Congregationalism, while the new church (the New England) increased in numbers and influence, and it finally be-

came one of the most important in the city.
It has since had several very able pastors,
Rev. S. C. Bartlett, D. D., afterwards professor in the seminary, Rev. Dr. J. G. Johnson, and others.

At this time the subject of establishing a
theological seminary in the interior was agi-
tating the minds of ministers in different
localities. In 1853 Rev. L. Smith Hobart
of Michigan prepared a plan for such an
institution of a somewhat unique form, which
was favorably considered by the General Association, but no steps were taken for carrying it into execution. In the following year,
Rev. Stephen Peet, of Batavia, near Chicago, conceived the idea of starting a seminary in Chicago, and, consulting his neighbor, Rev. G. S. F. Savage, they invited
others to meet them in the city. A convention was called which was largely attended,
at which it was decided to go forward with
the scheme. "Meanwhile," say the directors of the seminary, in their "Historical
Sketch," "the movement was begun and the
project was held before the churches by Rev.
J. C. Holbrook, in the *Congregational Herald*, of which he was the editor." A board
of directors was chosen, and a charter of

incorporation secured, and Rev. Mr. Peet was appointed financial agent. Only six of these directors were living in 1897, of whom I am the oldest.

Mr. Peet, the financial agent, entered heartily into the work of raising funds, in which he was successful. But in 1857 there occurred the memorable depression in business in the country, and it became problematical whether the enterprise of establishing the seminary could be carried out. At the triennial convention (1861) Mr. Olmstead, the treasurer, suggested that in view of the state and prospects of the finances it would perhaps be best to abandon the enterprise, and E. D. Holden, a prominent lay director, of Milwaukee, seconded the proposition. But the great majority said No. The directors in their report said, "There is a fear abroad that the seminary is in *peril of death*; and the terrible fact is that those fears are warranted." The salaries of the professors were not half paid, and a large debt had been incurred in the purchase of a location. Deacon Philo Carpenter, however, came to the rescue by gifts and change of location. He contributed $60,000 while living, and $55,000 by bequest; Mr. Keyes of Quincy gave a block in that city that netted about $12,000; Col. C. G. Hammond of Chicago gave about $50,000, and Dr. D. K. Pearson afterwards gave $230,000.

The plan of the lecture and reading terms was kept up for thirty years. Their special course in English was adopted, and there are German, Swedish, Norwegian, and Danish departments of great value, to provide ministers for the vast foreign population of the West.

The result has been the establishment of one of the most important institutions of the kind in our land, with several large and elegant buildings, and a faculty unsurpassed in ability by that of any other seminary of our own or any other denomination. After the death of Mr. Peet, Rev. A. S. Kedzie, of Michigan, was appointed financial agent, and for upwards of twelve years he served with great efficiency, largely increasing the endowment, and in other ways promoting the success of the enterprise.

The Chicago Theological Seminary is characterized by several peculiarities. One of these is its government. Instead of being controlled by a self-perpetuating and independent board of trustees, it has a board of directors, elected by a triennial convention of delegates from the churches of all the states of its constituency, so that it is responsible directly to them, and the proceedings of the board are brought into review every three years. At the convention before referred to, there was much discussion in regard to making the training of the students *practical*, and this was advocated by Messrs. Hobart and Peet, and has been virtually accomplished by arrangements for city missions, Chicago Commons, and the sociological department.

Says the "Historical Sketch," already referred to:

In the convention, some urged a special course of study, by which men, too old to go through college, or for other reasons unable to do so, yet nevertheless having had advantages of study, and having withal a heart devoted to the work, and natural gifts therefor, might be educated for the ministry. This course was advocated by Rev. J. C. Holbrook, suggested, perhaps, by his own successful experience, and as the course of other Christian denominations had suggested to many minds. The convention authorized this department of the seminary's work; and the usefulness of the men who have thereby been educated for the ministry has amply justified the wisdom of the convention. In its essential features, this course of study has been adopted by other theological seminaries.

I was one of the charter members of the institution and for several years, and until I left the West, a director. Rev. G. S. F. Savage, D. D., who has been secretary for thirty-six years, has been a very active and efficient worker for it, and to him is due much of the credit of its success. He has also been actively associated with all the measures for advancing Congregationalism in the West, from the Michigan City convention in 1846 till now, and has been a member of all the great conventions since the former.

For about two years, I continued to discharge the double duty of editor of the new paper and pastor of the new church, the most laborious period of my life. But at length I found myself too severely taxed for this purpose, and I was compelled to relinquish the charge of the church, and to devote myself exclusively to the paper. At the end of my third year in Chicago, I was visited by a prominent member of the Dubuque church, who was commissioned to endeavor to induce me to return and resume my former position as its pastor. He represented that trouble had arisen in the church, and that it had resulted in the secession of a considerable number of the members to form a second

Presbyterian church; that great discourage-
ment had arisen among the remaining members; that they felt that my return was
indispensable, and he begged me to yield to
their request, and to resume my former pastorate with them. This appeal touched my
heart, and I could not resist the claims of my
old and beloved flock. I therefore secured a
successor in the editorial chair, and with my
family returned again to Dubuque, and was
duly reinstalled by a council in my former
position.

Thus, having finished my peculiar work
in Chicago, and having been warmly welcomed back to my old field, I again resumed
my labors in Dubuque, and was cheered by
the renewed confidence awakened in the
church, and by the earnest coöperation of
the members of the congregation. During
this second pastorate we were favored with
several important revivals of religion, and I
was assisted in one of these by Rev. Zachary
Eddy, and in others by such noted evangel-
ists as Horatio Foote, O. Parker, and J. T.
Avery. The work in connection with the
last-named was very extensive. Mr. Avery
preached daily for several weeks with great
effect; and, as the result, there were a hundred

conversions, including quite a body of young men, who proved a very valuable acquisition to the church.

At that time I had a deacon who was fond of a joke, and on the Sunday morning on which this large number of persons was received into the church, he was standing in front of the edifice, a little before service, when a gentleman from Boston, passing by, inquired what church that was. Being told, and invited to enter, he was seated in the deacon's pew, and when I read the names of the candidates, and they filed out in the aisle to enter into covenant, the gentleman was much astonished at the sight, and whispering to the deacon, he inquired how many we usually received at a time in that church. "Oh," replied the deacon, "generally about a hundred," to the great amazement of the inquirer.

CHAPTER XV

Soon after my return to Dubuque from Chicago, we found it necessary to erect a new house of worship. Not only was that which we occupied too small to accommodate the increasing congregation, but it was situated on the main street of the city, and in the midst of business blocks, and a more quiet location was desirable. We were offered $20,000 for the site and building (the site, it will be remembered, cost originally only $250) which we accepted, and secured a location a little more retired from the noise and confusion of the former place. A subscription was also secured for $10,000, and with $30,000 we began the erection of a fine, spacious, modern edifice, not surpassed by any other then in the state, and which, with subsequent improvements, now stands in the front rank of church buildings in Iowa.

In the spring of 1859 I received an invita-

THE THIRD HOUSE.

tion to visit San Francisco, California, and supply the pulpit of the First Congregational church there, during the absence of the young pastor, who was going East, like Cœlebs, "in search of a wife." Obtaining leave of absence from my church for several months, I accepted the offer, and, proceeding to New York with my wife, we took the steamer for Aspinwall, and, crossing the isthmus, reëmbarked at Panama on another steamer, on the Pacific, reaching San Francisco after a pleasant passage of twenty-six days. There was then no transcontinental railroad. On the bright morning of March 17, 1859, we passed through the Golden Gate, and first set foot on California soil. How vividly do I recall the experiences of that trip!—the voyage down the Atlantic coast (it was my first sea voyage), the landing at Aspinwall, the crossing of the isthmus by rail, the reëmbarkation at Panama on the broad Pacific, the call at Acapulco, in Mexico, the passage through the Golden Gate, and the first sight of San Francisco, hemmed in, as it then was, by the sand hills on the west. One incident that occurred on the way was especially thrilling. A few days out of Panama we were aroused in the night by rappings on the window of our stateroom, and the cry, "The ship is on fire!" We and our neighbors were speedily gathered on the guards, and our consternation may be imagined as we gazed off upon the not far distant shores, barren, rocky and uninhabited, and wondered how we could subsist there, if we should be so happy as to reach them. Ere long, however, to our great relief, the fire was subdued, and we retired again to rest. The Sunday following our arrival I commenced my labors as temporary pastor, which continued until the following November, when my leave of absence was to expire.

I much enjoyed my connection with the First Church and congregation during the summer, and especially the opportunity afforded me to see the new and wonderful Golden State, only ten years after the grand rush of gold seekers to it from all parts of this land, and even of the world. Regularly, at the end of each month, I drew my salary, $200, in twenty-dollar pieces, and was at liberty to spend the intervening time between Sabbaths in trips, with my wife, to the various points of interest in the country.

How different then was what is now the great metropolis of the Pacific coast! There were then no street railways, no fine churches, none of the palatial residences and towering business blocks, and it was the terminus of no -railroad into the interior. One small ferry-boat plied across the bay to the little village of Oakland, a large part of the site of the present city being then covered with ever-green oaks.

"Whoever," wrote the celebrated Rev. Dr. Horace Bushnell of Hartford, after a visit to this state, " wishes for health's sake or for any other reason to change the sceneries or the objects and associations of his life, should set off, not for Europe, but for California. And this the more certainly if he is a sharp and loving observer of nature, for nature meets us there in moods entirely new. California is a new world, having its own combinations, characteristics, and colors."

Some of the excursions I made, accompanied by my wife, were of peculiar interest, and some account of them was published in The Pacific and in Eastern papers. From these I will give some extracts. These excursions were made, it will be remembered, while the country was yet new, and in a very different manner than they are now accomplished by railroads and coaches.

CHAPTER XVI

My first excursion, accompanied by my wife, was from San Francisco across the bay to Oakland and up the San José valley, in Alameda county, to the Mission, San José, where we first saw one of the quaint old edifices erected by the monks.

Another excursion was to the famous geysers in Napa county. Taking the little steamer plying between San Francisco and Petaluma, we reached the latter place about dusk. In the morning we took the stage, and, passing the pretty and lively little village of Santa Rosa at a distance of some twenty-five miles, we passed into the Russian River valley, which, we were then told, was the only section of the state in which Indian corn could be raised,—the crop which, in the middle West, we are accustomed to regard as a greater source of wealth than the gold mines of California, but of which we had seen no signs in our previous rambles. Now it may be often found elsewhere in the state. It was like seeing an old friend to look there on the stately form of Mondamin as we passed.

We left the stage at Ray's Station, at the foot of the mountain range where the geysers are found. Here we expected to take to the saddle. What was our dismay, on inquiry, to find that a party had preceded us and taken all the horses that were available! What was to be done? There were no accommodations for eating or sleeping, there being only one small hut with two 7 x 9 rooms. At length, however, the keeper of the station bethought himself of two old nags, one a mare, not in very good traveling condition. These we might have if we chose. We hesitated, but it was Hobson's choice, and we ordered them up. Two dilapidated saddles were found, and we mounted and set off up the mountain. It was past four o'clock in the afternoon, and there was a long, hard ride before us and no house on the way. But the moon was at the full, and we were told that the trail was plain, and as we had by this time become accustomed to California mountain life from previous trips, we did not fear, knowing that the worst that could befall us would be to be compelled to camp out in the bland climate, and go supperless to rest, minus a bed.

We soon found that we were in no danger of being run away with, for our nags were of the number of those (some human) who are born tired. They bore the whip bravely, and thus afforded us employment to beguile our way; but there was a fearful expenditure, on our part, of propelling power. It was something like riding a bicycle, only the propelling force was in the hands instead of the feet. Thus we toiled on, making what speed we could, an occasional descent helping to give impetus to our steeds; and just after nightfall we reached the end of the ridge from which we were to enter the canyon of the geysers.

The moon had risen and shone out brightly, so that we had no difficulty in keeping the trail down the steep declivity, and soon we could faintly distinguish the puffing of the great geyser, and began to perceive the sulphurous vapors that impregnated the air, which assured us that we were approaching our place of destination. Presently the cheerful light from the hotel windows broke on our sight, and, hastening on, we dismounted at the door. We were regaled with a bountiful supper, partly of game, and found comfortable quarters for the night.

In the morning we rose early and eagerly gazed from the windows of our chamber to behold our surroundings. Opposite to us, across the valley, rose a high, precipitous mountain, and near the foot of it we could see the vapors curling up from the boiling springs, which were themselves hidden from our view. After taking a sulphur bath in water drawn from the warm springs, and partaking of an excellent breakfast, we sallied forth to explore the locality and to examine the wonderful objects of curiosity congregated there. We found we were near the bottom of a deep mountain gorge or chasm, with sides from one thousand to fifteen hundred feet high, covered with a fine growth of evergreen timber. Through this gorge ran a small stream called the River Pluton. Crossing this, we followed a footpath up the opposite ascent, and soon reached some fissures in the rocks, from which issued clouds of steam from boiling springs below. This was "The Devil's Wash-tub." And, by the way, that personage seems to possess many localities, as we have found in various sections.

Turning now to the left, we beheld the

large body of vapor rising from the Great
Geyser. Following the trail, we reached
a projecting point called the " Mount of Fire,"
and from it gazed down into a deep cavity
called the " Devil's Canyon," and saw all
along, for a distance of an eighth of a mile
on both sides of the cavity, some fifty feet
deep, jets of vapor from a multitude of fissures filling the air with sulphurous odors.
After watching these operations for a short
time, we descended into the ravine, winding
our way cautiously where it was safe to tread,
and at length found ourselves in " The Chamber of Horrors." We soon reached the principal or " Steamboat Geyser," so called because it sends forth a noise resembling that
from the escape pipe of a high-pressure
steamer letting off steam. Standing on one
side of this Great Geyser, we shuddered to
think that the earth might give way beneath
us and plunge us into the burning abyss.
The heat was intense, and at a distance of
several feet we were in danger of scorching
our shoes.

A little further down we beheld a large
round basin in the rock, six or eight feet in
diameter and three or four deep, filled with
dark, sulphurous mud of the consistency of

paste or hasty pudding, heated to great intensity, and boiling and sputtering and throwing up jets in the liveliest manner. This is called by some "The Devil's Punch-bowl," and by others, "The Witch's Caldron."

All around us, as we passed on, we heard the hissing of steam, and found the earth heated to a high degree, and in some spots too soft to bear the tread of human foot, while on every side the air was charged with various suffocating gases, showing that there is a variety of ingredients commingled in the mysterious chambers below. In this immediate locality there is little or no vegetation, but not far off it appears to be wonderfully stimulated by the heat.

High mountains shut in the gorge, and innumerable empty cavities are seen, which are exhausted laboratories and extinct fountains. Altogether, large and small, there are not less than two hundred fissures, from which vapors issue, and, what is very remarkable, there are here congregated in immediate vicinage to each other springs of every degree of temperature, from very cold to the intensest heat, and containing a great variety of ingredients. Here are found pure alum, salt, and sulphur, and springs in which all are mingled, and others in which iron and manganese are added. Pure Epsom salts, alum, and sulphur can be gathered here by handfuls. What a grand natural laboratory is this!

The geysers were discovered in 1847 by a hunter. They were visited by Professor Forest Shephard in 1850 or 1851. He and his party from Napa valley reached the peak of the mountain overlooking the Geyser canyon one morning, and he thus describes what he saw:

Immediately at our feet there opened an immense chasm, apparently formed by the rending of the mountain. The sun's rays had penetrated into the narrow valley, and so lighted up the dark defile, that, from a distance of four or five miles, we distinctly saw dense columns of steam rising from the banks of the little river Pluton. It was with difficulty we could persuade ourselves that we were not looking down upon some manufacturing city, until by a tortuous descent we arrived at the spot where, at once, the secret of the inner world opened upon our astonished senses. In the space of half a mile we discovered some two hundred openings, through which steam issued with violence to the height of 150 to 200 feet. The roar of the largest tube could be heard for a mile or more, and the sharp hissing of the smaller ones is still ringing in my ears. Numerous cones are formed by the accumulations of various salts and deposits of sulphur crystals. Some of the cones appear to be immense boiling caldrons, and you hear the lashing and foaming gyrations beneath your feet. Curiosity impels you forward—fear holds you back; and while you are hesitating, the thin crust beneath your feet gives way, and you feel yourself sinking into the fiery maelstrom below.

The rocks around are rapidly dissolving under the metamorphic action. Porphyry and jasper are transformed into a kind of potter's clay. Granite is rendered soft. Feldspar is partly converted into alum, and wood is silicified or changed into lignite. In this connection, finding some drops of a very dense fluid, highly refractive, I was led to believe that pure carbon might crystallize and form the diamond. Unfortunately, I lost the precious drop. Multitudes of grizzly bears used formerly to make their beds on the warm ground, and panthers, deer, hares, and squirrels would take up their winter quarters in the very midst of the geyser mounds.

Such are the geysers. We spent two days in this interesting spot, and bathed in natural sulphur baths, and wandered about the locality. Remounting our horses, we retraced our way by the tortuous bridle path to Ray's Station. On the way, early that memorable morning, we were favored with the sight of a glorious sunrise such as I have never seen surpassed except once—from the top of Mount Washington in the New Hampshire White Mountains. Far off in the distance was the Russian River valley, covered with a dense fog rising from the stream, which gave the appearance of a beautiful lake, whose waters were rolling in billows, while here and there were seen the lofty conical hilltops, which rose above the fog, resembling islands. It was a complete optical illusion, and we could hardly persuade ourselves that we were not looking upon a vast sheet of water. At eight o'clock we reached Ray's—just in time to catch the stage for Napa, where we spent a day. The next morning, early, we hired a horse and buggy and passed down through the far-famed valley to Napa City, where we embarked in a steamer for San Francisco. The early ride down that valley I shall never forget. I thought I had seen a bit of Paradise in the San José valley, but Napa even exceeded that in beauty. The road ran through its center, and was as level as a house floor, and almost as hard as if it were macadamized. The valley was one continuous wheat-field, yellow with the ripening grain; evergreen oaks, with long pendant branches, were scattered through it; the air was fresh and balmy in the early morning; the meadow-lark sang his matin song, and everything combined to exhilarate the spirits and charm the eye and ear. And so ended a delightful week.

CHAPTER XVII

The most laborious and at the same time the most interesting excursion that we made on that memorable summer was to the far-famed Yosemite Valley. We were fortunate enough to visit it at an early period, and to see it in its pristine state, and before it had undergone many changes and improvements(?).

Comparatively few had preceded us, and I believe I preached the first sermon that was ever delivered in it. There was then no railroad to relieve the fatigue of any part of the journey, nor even a carriage road for a considerable part of the way. Our route was by steamer to Stockton, and thence by stage sixty miles to Coulterville. Beyond this place there were no public conveyances, and, associating ourselves with several young gentlemen, we mounted hardy and sure-footed mustangs, and with a mounted guide and a pack mule to carry our carpetbags, blankets, cooking utensils, and provisions, we formed a grotesque group, as dressed for the expedition we emerged from the little village to plunge into the wilderness. Twenty miles brought us to Black's ranch for the night, the last habitation before reaching the valley.

At 5 o'clock the next morning we again mounted our horses for a long and hard day's ride. Our path was a narrow bridle trail, up steep mountain sides, over precipitous spurs, through deep gorges and ravines, and dense forests, in which we saw no living things but lizards, while the silence was most profound, unbroken by even the twitter of a bird. At length, having traveled forty miles that day, we reached the point where the trail descended into the valley. And such a descent! It was truly appalling. We were 5,000 feet above sea level, and 3,500 above that of the valley below. The path was not more than a foot wide, and ran in a zigzag course down the mountain side. My wife was secured from falling over her horse's head by a strap which kept her in her seat. Preceded by our guide and the pack mule, we screwed our courage up, and, allowing our steeds to pick their way, we at length reached the bottom of the descent, almost too exhausted to retain our seats, and looked back to survey the steep declivity and indulge a feeling of gratitude that the feat was safely accomplished.

Following then the bank of the charming crystal Merced River, which runs through the whole length of the valley, amidst a verdant, grassy meadow, at the end of five miles, tired almost beyond endurance, we reached our stopping-place for the night. That night was one long to be remembered. We took our evening meal in a canvas tent, for there was no house at that time in the valley, and then cast about for a place to sleep. There were no inhabitants there, but I secured a bed, such as it was, for my wife, in a rough board shanty occupied by a family that had arrived a few days before to keep a sort of tavern, the woman being the only one within fifty or sixty miles of the place. For myself a bed of shavings and a blanket under the branches of some trees formed my resting-place, where I slept as soundly as any crowned head under the silken canopy of his downy couch. It was a glorious night, the heavens were clear, stars shone out brightly, and a full moon illuminated the valley. Directly opposite, and in full view, half a mile distant, the great Yosemite Fall poured its foaming waters down a precipice nearly 3,000 feet high, and by its monotonous thunder helped to lull me to sleep. That was my first night in this weird spot, and you may imagine my feelings as I tried to realize where I was, far up in the Sierras, and among some of the most wonderful scenes of nature to be found on earth.

In the morning, refreshed with sleep in this cool and bracing atmosphere, we were ready to explore the wonders of the place. The valley derives its name from a tribe of Indians. It is some ten miles in length, running in a due east and west direction, so that the sun rises at one end and sets at the other, casting into it his cheering beams all day long. It is a vast rift of the Sierra Nevadas, and forms a natural curiosity of which no adequate impression can be given by mere description. I had read about it, and conversed with those who had visited it, but I had no just conception of it until I saw it. If there were no falls it would be worth a thousand miles' travel to see its towering rocks and mountain peaks enclosing a lovely meadow, and the meandering river winding its way at its own sweet will. But there are falls congregated there such as can be seen nowhere else.

Standing in one place, you seem to be in the midst of a perfect amphitheater, and you are reminded of Dr. Johnson's Happy Valley in Rasselas. Indeed, his description almost tallies with this view. As you pass through the valley you see numerous peaks of fantastic forms, resembling well-known objects, and named accordingly.

Passing up the valley from where we entered it, we beheld the first graceful waterfall, the Bridal Veil, on the right. A little further on, at the left, the huge promontory of rock called El Capitan rises, of smooth, grey granite, 3,090 feet high, or three fifths of a mile, and so perpendicular that a marble dropped from the top at the length of a man's arm, would not touch it before reaching the ground. Think of standing at its base and looking at its top, seven times as high as the dome of St. Peter's at Rome! What a pigmy does one seem to himself to be in such a position, and how insignificant do all human works appear by the comparison! Further up the valley are the twin peaks called "The Brothers," and then comes another, shaped like a tower, and on its round front appears what looks like a clock-face, with hands pointing to half-past six. At the extreme upper end of the valley are the two domes, the loftiest of all, one of them 3,729 feet high, while opposite to it the other rises to a height of 4,593 feet. The original mass had fallen away from some convulsion, leaving these peaks standing, and had dammed the river below, forming a beautiful lake. Here was the traditionary home, according to the Indians, of the guardian of the valley. On the face of one dome are the outlines of a crowned head—Tu-tock-a-nula, and the Indian tradition is that this was the name of the last presiding spirit, and that he carved the outlines of his noble head upon the face of the rock.

But the waterfalls—not one only, but six—are all different, and exceedingly beautiful. I have already referred to one, the Bridal Veil, formed by a small river with a descent iuto the valley on the side of 925 feet, which forms a spray resembling the delicate fabric of which ladies' veils are made. Some miles further up the valley is the Vernal Fall, where the whole volume of the Merced River tumbles over a ledge of rocks, perpendicularly, 600 feet. Still further up the same stream is the Nevada Fall, 700 feet in height. But the grandest of all these falls is the Yosemite, not on the Merced, but on a stream that rises high up in the Sierras, which, reaching the side of the valley, pitches itself by three grand leaps over a precipice 2,500 feet high, the first leap being 1,500, the second 400, and the last 600. This, in its totality, is the highest known waterfall in the world. Niagara is only 160 feet, though, of course, with a far larger volume of water; Passaic is 70, the falls of the Nile are 40, and some in the Alps 1,000. But think of this, half a mile high! Looking up from the bottom, the stream at the top, fifty feet wide, appears to be not more than eighteen inches. While fording this stream near the foot of this fall, my wife's horse suddenly lay down in the middle of it, compelling her to slide off into the water, which, fortunately, was not deep. The guide having brought out the horse, she remounted, suffering no serious inconvenience in the dry and warm atmosphere, and we proceeded on our course.

Such is a very inadequate description of this wonderful valley. A gentleman who spent the Fourth of July there the season previous to our visit, witnessed a thunder storm, of which he said "the effect no words can describe."

> "From crag to crag
> Leaped the live thunder—
> Not from one lone cloud,
> But every mountain found a tongue."

Rev. Dr. Anderson, pastor of the First Presbyterian Church in San Francisco, when I asked him if it was worth while to visit the valley, said:

MY DEAR SIR,—You had better go if it were to cost you a thousand dollars. I have traveled in Europe from the Alps to Perth in Hungary, and I never saw anything equal to it. I certainly miss there the glaciers of Chamouni, but I know of no single wonder on earth that can claim a superiority to the Yosemite. Just imagine yourself for one hour in a vast chasm nearly ten miles long, with ingress and egress for birds, and water at either extremity, and none elsewhere except at three points—up the sides 3,000 to 4,000 feet high, the chasm scarcely more than a mile wide, with walls of mainly naked and perpendicular gray granite, so that looking up to the sky is like looking out of an unfathomable profound—and you will have some conception of the Yosemite.

Says another clergyman, who has visited the Alps, and found no parallel:

And what shall I say when standing in the valley a mile wide? You know that if those granite walls should fall towards each other, they would smite their foreheads together hundreds of feet above where you stand.

We spent four days in the valley, and could have enjoyed as many more in exploring its wonders, had we not been compelled to bid it adieu. To avoid so long and hard a horseback ride on our return as when we went up, we left the valley about three o'clock P. M., by the same trail by which we entered, and spent the night at the top of the ridge under shelter of some noble evergreen trees. Our guide picketed the horses while I kindled a fire and put on the kettle for a tin cup of the beverage that " cheers but not inebriates." We then spread our blankets on a bed of hemlock boughs, and went to rest on the bosom of mother earth. The next morning we were in the saddle again at five o'clock, and stopping only to lunch at noon, we spent the night again at Black's, and the next day at Coulterville. We took the stage for Stockton and the steamer for San Francisco, where we again found ourselves in the midst of the hum and hurry and thronged streets of the city, quite in contrast with the

10

natural grandeur and solitude of the valley we had lately left.

The influence of such scenes as we had witnessed is most salutary on a reflective mind. Says Bryant:

> To him who in the love of nature
> Holds communion with her visible forms,
> She speaks a various language.

And she ever proclaims the power and wisdom and goodness of the glorious Mind that designed a world so full of innumerable forms of grandeur and beauty.

> There's nothing bright, above, below,
> From flowers that bloom to stars that glow,
> But in its light my soul can see
> Some features of the Deity.

It is not a wild fancy that God himself takes pleasure in the beauties of the works of creation. Charles Kingsley, in his book on the West Indies, after describing some curious and wonderful productions of nature says:

There are those that will smile at my superstition if I state my belief that He who ordained the laws of nature had as one end in view that he might delight himself in the beauty of some of these creations. Be it so. If so, their minds are differently constituted from mine.

CHAPTER XVIII

On another occasion we took a steamer for Sacramento, and, visiting the State fair, were much surprised by the evidence afforded of the resources and progress of the then new state. The pyramids of mammoth squashes, some weighing 250 pounds each, and other vegetable products, astounded us, and served, in a measure, to prepare us to behold the gigantic denizens of the "Big Tree Grove" (the California term), which were the ultimate objects of our trip.

Taking the stage from the capital city for Mokelumne Hill, we mounted horses at the latter place for a solitary ride across a mountain ridge covered with a dense forest. Our course was on a narrow trail difficult to follow, and we were often at a loss as to the right way, but at length we came in sight of the Mammoth Tree Hotel in the edge of the grove. The approach to the house was between two noble specimens of the trees, which stood about fifteen feet apart and were called "The Guardsmen." One was twenty and the other twenty-two feet in diameter, and sixty and sixty-six feet in circumference, respectively. They rose to the height of 300 feet, that is, 100 feet higher than Trinity Church steeple in New York city, and were as straight as an arrow.

The discovery of the big trees was made by a hunter named Dowd, who was employed by a water company to procure meat for their workmen. One day, while Dowd was pursuing a grizzly bear which he had wounded, he suddenly came upon one of these immense trees and was amazed at the sight. He forgot his bear, and, stopping in mid-career, he stepped back and surveyed it with his eye and then walked around it and estimated its height and circumference, and then took his way back to camp. He told the men what he had seen, but was only laughed at for his Munchausen story, and was told that the fright caused by the bear had disordered his vision. Subsequently, he induced some of the men to go with him, ostensibly in quest of a wounded grizzly, and leading the way he was soon able to point out the tree, and then exclaimed, "There is the grizzly I spoke of!" The story soon spread and the existence of the grove was ascertained, which has since been a place of resort for visitors from all parts of the state and the land. The whole area occupied by it is about fifty acres, and there are nearly one hundred full grown specimens of the species. Twenty of them exceed twenty-five feet in diameter.

Leaving the hotel after resting a little from the fatigue of the horseback ride, we entered a canvas tent and beheld an enormous stump, the top of which was about seven feet from the ground. This had been smoothed off like a floor, and around the outer edge were arranged seats. We were told that dancing parties had occupied this floor, and that on one occasion four sets of cotillions of eight persons each, or thirty-two in all, used it at once, while at another time the troupe of Alleghanian singers gave a concert upon it to an audience of fifty persons! Stepping across it, I found it was ten paces in diameter, or about thirty feet. Hardly believing it, I walked around the outside and assured myself by a survey that it was a veritable tree stump, the roots still fixed in the ground. Skepticism then vanished. Realizing that my statements as to the size of this tree might seem to be incredible, I took the precaution to procure a string, which was carried around the stump, and in lecturing to my congregation in Dubuque on my return home I stood on the platform and held one end of the string, while the other was carried around the large room in which I was speaking. It nearly reached around it, and inclosed a large part of the audience. While this was in progress, amid constant outbursts of laughter, there was at last a grand cheer as the real truth as to the dimensions of the tree was realized.

On one side of the stump lay the tree which had been felled, and the top of its sides reached as high as the eaves of the house. On one side a ladder with twenty-six steps was placed by which to ascend upon it. Reaching the top by this, I began to wonder how this tree was felled, and was told that some years before some vandals resolved upon the act; but to attempt to accomplish it with axe or saw was useless, and so they employed a number of augers of large size, and fifteen feet long, with which they bored a series of holes around it, but still it refused to fall. At length another large tree was felled against it, and it came down with a tremendous crash, the noise reverberating through the forest like thunder, startling the birds from their eyries and the beasts from their lairs.

> With sudden roar the aged monarch falls ;
> One crash, the death hymn of the perfect tree.
> Low lies the plant to whose creation went
> Sweet influence from every element :
> Whose living towers the years conspired to build,
> Whose giddy top the morning loved to gild.

Five men were occupied twenty-five days in accomplishing the overthrow. It was the very tree the hunter, Dowd, first discovered. And yet, large as it was, it was not *the* big tree of the group.

Leaving this point, we took the tour of the grove, and following the prescribed path, and entering the shadows, we looked around with awe and reverence as we beheld the lofty trees towering upward towards the heavens, and were reminded of Bryant's noble forest hymn :

> The groves were God's first temples ;   *   *   *
> Amidst the cool and silence man knelt down
> And offered to the Mightiest, solemn thanks
> And supplications.   Ah, why
> Should we, in the world's riper years, neglect
> God's ancient sanctuaries and adore
> Only among the crowd and under roofs
> That our frail hands have made?

The principal trees of the group had received fanciful names, which were affixed to them by labels, with the dimensions of each. One whose vast trunk had been burned out, though still standing, was called "The Miner's Cabin." Three others, in close proximity, were "The Graces"; then, further on, "The Old Bachelor," a forlorn specimen, 298 feet high, with rents in the bark, symbolic of the dilapidated garments of its namesake, showing the inconvenience of single life; then "The Old Maid," stiff and firm, the spinster of the family, at a respectful distance from the Bachelor, and all her foliage gathered in a tuft, like a cap, at the top. "The Husband and Wife" seemed affectionately leaning towards each other for a chaste kiss, as their branches interlocked. But "Hercules" was the largest and finest specimen of standing trees, estimated to contain 725,000 feet of lumber, or enough to make a good-sized raft. "The Father," enfeebled by age, had been blown down some years before, and we traversed the hollow trunk inside for two hundred feet in an erect position, as if going through some vast tunnel. Through a knot-hole on one side visitors make their egress, illustrative of receding from an untenable position or "creeping out of a knot-hole." The circumference of this tree is 110 feet, giving a diameter of 33 feet. When standing, it rose to the height of 450 feet. This seems almost incredible, as the height of the dome of St. Peter's at Rome, the highest in the world, is only the same.

But the greatest wonder of all was the horseback ride lengthwise through the trunk of a huge old tree, once overthrown by the wind. About seventy-five feet in length of the prostrate trunk had been burned out, and through that length visitors rode on horseback without stooping, as I did myself. This gives, perhaps, the most striking idea of the vast dimensions of these trees.

As I was delivering a lecture on this subject in a certain town, after my return home, there was a lady in the audience who sat and listened with amazement to my descriptions until I reached this point of the horseback ride, when, drawing a long breath, she turned to a gentleman at her side and whispered, as I afterwards learned, "I suppose we must believe all this, for it is a minister that says it."

Walking about through the grove, our guide pointed out a young specimen of the species about two feet high. The contrast was ludicrous between it and its giant neighbors two or three thousand years old, perhaps, and we could not help laughing at the idea of this little fellow starting thus in the race of life, with high hopes and lofty ambition to rival his parent and uncles and aunts so many hundred feet high. But we bade him God-speed, and no doubt, if he perseveres, he will, in time, stand as loftily erect as his relatives, and some two thousand years hence be as great an object of curiosity as they. But what a length of time to wait for his maturity!

It is difficult to convey the idea of the size of these trees to one who has not seen them. As to the height, think of a church steeple of 150 feet, and yet it is only half the height of some of them, and one third of that of the highest. For the size, a board 200 feet long might be sawed from the center of one trunk which, set on edge, would cover the whole front of a block of two-story houses.

As to the age of some of these trees. A correspondent of the London *Times* calculated it to be 6,408 years, reaching back to the times of Adam. But no doubt there was a mistake in the data of his calculation. But from counting the rings they have been supposed to be from 2,000 to 3,000 years old at least.[1]   No castle in Europe is half as antiquated.   They were hoary at the period of the crusades.   But one thing only is more awe-inspiring—the great pyramid of Egypt.   Says Dr. Bushnell: "We enter where these majestic minarets are crowded as in some city of pilgrimage, there to look, for the first time, in silent awe at the mere life principle."   Says another:

Their age unknown.   In what depths of time
Might fancy wander sportively and deem
Some monarch of this grove set forth
His tiny shoot, when primeval flood
Receded, or perhaps, coeval with Assyrian kings,
His branches in dominion spread; from age
To age his sapling heirs with empire grew.
While art and science slept, their sturdy younglings throve,
And in their turn rose when Columbus
Gave to Spain a world.

A church spire has been called a finger pointing to heaven.   So these trees prompt the language of devotion—

Father, Thy hand
Hath reared these venerable columns.

[1] We have the great authority of Professor Whitney and Asa Gray that the sequoia of California have attained more than two thousand years of age. See an article by Asa Gray in Johnson's Cyclopedia, 2d edition, vol. 7, p. 133.

My heart is awed within me when I think
Of the great miracle that still goes on
In silence round me—the perpetual work
Of Thy creation finished and yet renewed
Forever.   Written on Thy works I read
The lesson of Thine own eternity.

CHAPTER XIX

We visited several localities where the pro-
cess of hydraulic mining was in operation,
and were astonished at its extent and at the
expense of money and labor involved. There
were miles on miles of flumes or aqueducts
along the hillsides and across deep canyons,
to bring the necessary immense quantities of
water. So vast were the excavations created
with this water that the soil carried into the
rivers below was found eventually to be an
obstruction to navigation, and a law was
passed to prevent the filling up of the streams.
It seemed as if Titans had been at work tear-
ing up the earth and leveling the hills. Millions on millions of gold were extracted. It
was worth a long journey to witness the
results of human enterprise, labor, and pecuniary outlay in the greedy search for gold.

At that time Rev. W. C. Pond was performing self-sacrificing work as a home missionary at Downieville, an important mining locality in the same region. We wished to visit him. The place was in a deep valley, surrounded on all sides by mountains, and no carriage or wagon road had been constructed to afford access to it. Everything there had been carried in on the backs of mules. One of these animals had been killed in conveying an iron safe into the place, and the sole piano (and there *was* one there) was lowered down one of the sides of the valley by ropes, as the only mode of getting it there. As the single way of reaching the place was on mule backs, we procured a couple of those useful animals at the nearest stage station where we were stopping, and, thus mounted, followed the very narrow ascending trail along the side of a mountain, and, after a long and fatiguing ride, descended into the town and were greeted by the missionary at his house.

It was rather a perilous ride, as the track was barely wide enough for a single mule to pass over it, and a misstep on his part might precipitate both him and his rider down the precipice. Such accidents rarely happened, however, with such sure-footed and sagacious beasts, although, not long before, a heavily loaded one thus fell and was killed, either from a misstep or from being crowded off by a train going in an opposite direction. This meeting of trains was one source of danger, and it required great caution when it happened, especially if it was where no provision had been made for such an exigency by excavations in the side of the mountain. We spent two or three days in Downieville, including a Sabbath when I preached. We not only enjoyed our visit, but were enabled to cheer the lonely minister and his excellent wife by our presence.

One other excursion only of this very interesting season I will mention. My brother-in-law, Dr. Clark, being desirous of giving the finishing touch to our impression of the beauties of the state, procured a lively pair of horses and a carriage, and, with his wife, gave us a sweeping tour around the south end of the magnificent bay of San Francisco. Proceeding up the west side, stopping at one of the palatial residences on the way and refreshing ourselves with luscious grapes from its great conservatory, liberally presented by the proprietor, a friend of the Doctor's, we spent the night at San José, the Garden City. The next morning we drove to New Almaden and explored the quicksilver mine there with much interest. Returning down the east side of the bay, through the beautiful San José valley, to Oakland, we crossed the ferry to the city, after a most delightful trip of several days, and not long after began making preparations for our departure for home.

On the 5th of November we embarked on the steamer for Panama, and crossing the isthmus by rail and reëmbarking again at Aspinwall, we were in New York after a passage of twenty-six days. We, however, had another experience of danger, even more exciting than that occasioned by the fire on shipboard on our way out. In the Gulf of Tehuantepec we were overtaken by a severe storm in the night and were in imminent danger of foundering. The sea swept over the decks and carried away much of the live stock on board, and the captain said that at one time he feared he should be obliged to cut away the upper deck, on which was our stateroom. But our stout ship weathered the storm and carried us safely through to Panama. On reaching home we were warmly welcomed by our church and congregation, and I settled down again to my work.

Thus ended one of the most enjoyable, if not the most useful, seasons of my life. I hope I did some good while in California, and I am sure I derived much personal benefit from my visit. When a few years subsequently I visited Europe, I was thankful that I had seen the wonders of California. It is related of the celebrated Robert Hall, the eloquent English Baptist preacher, that he was once visited by an American, and it came out in conversation that he (the visitor) had never seen Niagara Falls. So astonished and disgusted was Mr. Hall to learn the fact that a man should go abroad without having seen such a wonder in his own land, that he turned away and would have nothing more to do with him. And so I felt, when abroad, that I should have been ashamed if I had not seen this part of my own country before crossing the Atlantic to see other lands. And I remember that when Rev. Dr. J. P. Thompson of New York gave me a letter of introduction to ministers in London, I was surprised to find that he mentioned particularly that I had visited California, which he probably thought would help to recommend me to their regard.

After my return home I never lost my interest in the state, and always hoped some time to make my residence there. I was glad, then, when the way opened for my return, and I am thankful that it has fallen to my lot to spend my last days in its genial clime and to be associated with so excellent and sympathetic a band of ministerial brethren as are here to be found. It is a privilege to lend what little aid I can towards building up the kingdom of God in the Empire State of the West.

How little conception there is not only among us, but in our country at large, of the vast future that is in store for the regions bordering on the Pacific Ocean! In 1852 William H. Seward in a speech in the United States Senate uttered this prophecy :

Henceforth European commerce, European politics, European thought, and European activity, although actually becoming more intimate, will, nevertheless, sink relatively in importance; while the Pacific Ocean, its shores, its islands, and the regions beyond will become the chief theatre of events in the world's great hereafter.

Taking this for his text, Mr. Thurston, Hawaiian minister to the United States, published in the *North American Review* a most able and interesting article in which he corroborates Mr. Seward's prediction by pointing out the vast prospective importance of all the countries in and around the Pacific, Australia, Japan, China, Siberia, the multitude of the islands which have been appropriated by European powers and their various resources, Mexico, Central America, and the Western South American countries, with the western slope of our own land and British Columbia. He especially enumerates the vast resources of California and closes with these words:

Prophesying is a dangerous and uncertain business, but it seems altogether probable that within ten or fifteen years the railroad across vast, and as yet undeveloped, Siberia, from St. Petersburg to Vladivostok, will have been completed, and that lines of steamships will radiate from the latter place to Vancouver, San Francisco, the Nicaragua canal, Australia, and the other southern colonies. The railroad system of the United States will have been extended to Alaska on the north and Chile on the south. The Nicaragua canal will have been completed, and a large portion of the enormous commerce that now pours through the Suez canal will have been diverted to it. Honolulu will be the centre of a cable system extending to Tahiti, Australia, Japan, Vancouver and San Francisco; while between all the main ports of the Pacific steamers of the size and speed of those plying between New York and Europe will be in use. The Pacific has already made giant strides of progress, but it is yet only on the threshold of the destiny that looms before it.

I commend this article to all who feel an interest in the great state of California, and the Pacific coast of our country. Rev. Dr. Barrows said at New Haven, "To the west of California is that Asiatic world of immeasurable greatness which, when awakened out of sleep, will combine with America to make the Pacific Ocean the chief highway of the world's commerce."

On our way out to San Francisco, we had for a fellow-traveler a lady from New York, with two very bright and interesting daughters, one four and a half years of age, and the other six. While in San Francisco the mother died, and, as we had become much interested in the children, we were permitted to adopt them. We reared and educated them, and were rewarded by seeing them develop into fine and useful women. The elder of them married a merchant of Stockton, California, Mr. E. B. Noble, where she now resides; the other became the wife of a gentleman of Minneapolis, Minnesota, Mr. W. S. Amsden, where she subsequently died. Both early became Christians. The elder has two daughters, and the other left two sons, and all give promise of being useful members of society. Never was a mother

more devoted to, and faithful in, the training of her own children than was my wife
to these, our adopted daughters, and she
regarded this as a very important part of
her life-work.

On my return from California, I resumed my
labors at Dubuque at a period of great excitement in the country, just preceding the
breaking out of the War of the Rebellion. I
found the people of the city and vicinity
under the full influence of that excitement.
The city and county formed a stronghold of
Democracy, many of the inhabitants being
from the South. The struggle was going
on between the Free-soilers and the friends of
slavery for the possession of Kansas; Lincoln and Douglas had their great debate,
and the forebodings of the War of the Rebellion were in the air. I felt called on, therefore, to bear my part in the controversy that
was shaking the country from end to end,
and accordingly preached many sermons on
slavery and the questions at issue to crowded
audiences, some of which were printed and
circulated.

When the war finally broke out, I advocated the emancipation of the slaves and the
enlistment of colored soldiers, and I ad-

dressed the first regiment of soldiers who were encamped in the suburbs. It is, I may here mention, a notable fact, unparalleled elsewhere, that Iowa furnished a regiment called "The Gray Beards," composed of men past the military age. A member of my church was chosen colonel, and they performed garrison duty, and thus enabled younger men to enter the field for active service. It was said that my pulpit spoke with no uncertain sound, and I was fully sustained by my loyal church. It is to the credit of the state of Iowa that it furnished its full quota of soldiers for the war, and never faltered or wavered in the support of the Federal Union.

CHAPTER XX

At length, after seven years' service in my second pastorate in Dubuque, occurred another providential interference in my affairs. The trustees of Iowa College found it necessary to solicit aid for that institution, which was regarded as so important to the state, and they fixed upon me as the proper person to visit New England to raise the modest sum of $2,000. My church granted me leave of absence for the purpose, and regarding it as of great importance that this, our denominational and Christian college should be sustained, I consented to undertake the task, and soon succeeded in securing the amount. My success, as is often the case, stimulated the trustees to enlarge their plan and increase the amount asked for to $5,000, and they urged me to continue the work of solicitation. I acceded to the request, and was again so successful that the duty of securing an endowment for the presidency of the college was laid upon me. Rev. G. F. Magoun had been elected to the office, but he declined to enter upon its duties until an endowment was obtained. This seemed to me to be a plain indication of Providence that I should make the effort to obtain it, and in this I was confirmed by the earnest request that I should do so by the secretary of the college society at the East, Rev. Theron Baldwin, D. D., who offered the endorsement of the movement by the society, which was afterwards given. But I foresaw that considerable time would be required for the purpose, and I felt that my church would suffer if left pastorless so long. I therefore asked to be released from my relation to it, and a council was called, which recommended my dismissal to undertake the work. The church acquiesced, and I removed, with my family, to Boston.

I felt that I was entering upon a laborious and uninviting task, but I was convinced of its great importance, and that I was called to it, not only by my brethren, but also by the voice of God. I began my work in Boston, and in its prosecution visited most of the leading churches in eastern Massachusetts, in Connecticut, in Providence, Rhode Island, and some in Maine, and was everywhere welcomed to the Congregational pulpits, and encouraged with liberal subscriptions. One or two incidents which occurred in my experience are of interest, and may be recorded.

There was a benevolent leather merchant in Boston who took great interest in my mission, and subscribed $500. Some time afterwards I was passing his store, and he was standing in the doorway. He called me into his counting-room, and asked to see my subscription book. I handed it to him, when he remarked: "I have lately met with a heavy pecuniary loss, and I have been thinking that it is a providential indication that I have not been giving enough," and thereupon sat down at his desk and changed the figures of his subscription from $500 to $1,000. Was not this correct reasoning, and was it not an example worthy of consideration by other business men?

I was aware that Mr. Samuel Williston, of Easthampton, Mass., was a very benevolent man, that he had given liberally to Amherst college, and that he preferred to select some one or more important objects to which to confine his gifts, rather than to scatter them promiscuously to several. Accordingly, I visited his place of residence, and on Saturday called on the pastor of his church and told him my errand, and asked the use of his pulpit on the Sabbath, to present my object. He very cordially acceded to my request, and I addressed his. congregation, Mr. Williston being present. At the close of the service Mr. Williston invited me to spend the evening at his house, as he wished to make some inquiries in regard to my object, and I accordingly did so.   His pastor, in a talk I had with him the day before, had advised me not to ask Mr. Williston for any small sum, as, if I did so, he would very likely be disposed not to give much attention to the subject.   I therefore decided that I would ask Mr. Williston to endow the presidency of the college, which had been fixed at $50,000.

I spent the evening very pleasantly with him and his wife, who was in entire sympathy with him in his benevolent operations. I answered their inquiries as to the importance and prospects of the college, and suggested that, if he were so disposed, it would be a most worthy opportunity for him to exercise his benevolence by endowing the chair of the presidency.   He, however, made no definite reply, but said he was going the next morning to Northampton, and invited me to take a seat with him in his chaise, and then he would tell me what he would do. The next morning he called for me, and we set out. During the ride, he said he had considered the matter, and had decided to give me his note for $10,000, as he had not the money just then at command, and that he would add $10,000 more at a subsequent time. He gave me his note, and it was paid not long after, with the other $10,000. A year or two afterwards he added $8,500 more to complete the endowment of the presidency of the college, I having collected enough from other sources to make up the balance. I hold the receipt of the treasurer for $42,-500, remitted by me, including the $20,000 from Mr. Williston. Thus I fulfilled my mission for the college, and virtually secured, in fact, the whole sum which I was expected to raise.

While engaged in this work, quite unexpectedly to me, it was announced that Williams college, then under the presidency of Dr. Mark Hopkins, had bestowed on me the honorary degree of Doctor of Divinity, and soon I was officially notified of the fact. This I did not suppose was done with the idea that I was a profound theologian, for I made no pretensions to be that, but as a recognition of the fact that I was a devoted pastor, and earnestly endeavoring to discharge faithfully the duties of that office, in virtue of which I was, actually, a *Doctor Divinitatis*, that is, a teacher of divine truth. I did not decline the honor. Had I done so, it seems to me it would have savored of conceit, and manifested a desire to distinguish myself from the great number of those who had accepted it before me.

While prosecuting my mission for the college, I received an invitation to supply the pulpit of the Congregational church, in Homer, New York, and to present my appeal for the institution. I did so, and preached twice on the Sabbath. After services, I was requested to remain over the next day to meet the trustees and deacons of the church and society, in the evening. I did so, and was then asked if I would accept a call to the pastorate. I replied that I would, provided I might have two or three months to finish my work for the college. This was assented to, and I at once removed my family there, and was subsequently installed in office by an ecclesiastical council, after accomplishing my mission in behalf of the college.

CHAPTER XXI

THE CONGREGATIONAL CHURCH AT HOMER,
N. Y.—LABORS THERE—A NEW MISSION

The Congregational church of Homer has had a remarkable history. It is one of the oldest, if not the oldest, of the order in the state of New York. The first settlers of the town were from Massachusetts and Connecticut, in 1793, and they brought with them the habits and opinions prevailing in those states. At first there were but six families, but they established public worship on the first Sabbath, and it is said, on good authority, that there has never been an omission of the service to this day. In early days central New York was to a great extent godless, intemperate, and schoolless, and it was a common saying to new immigrants, " If you wish to settle among religionists, go to Homer." The church was organized soon after the opening of this century, and when I became its pastor was one of the largest churches in the state outside of New York and Brooklyn, and had a fine brick house of worship. The place had ever been noted for its moral, religious, and material prosperity.

At an early day an academy was established in the village, largely by the influence of members of this church, which has always maintained a high character, and of which Samuel Woolworth, LL. D., afterwards Secretary of the Board of Regents of New York, was for many years principal. For a long period, students resorted to this institution from all parts of western and central New York, and some of the most eminent men in the ministry of the Congregational and Presbyterian denominations, as well as others of high position in political life, are among the alumni of this school. There were at one time *four* United States Senators who had been in part educated here. It has always been under a strongly evangelical religious influence. The town has been favored with many revivals of religion and the people have been more than ordinarily intelligent, as well as moral.

One incident in the early history of the church is worth recording, and I give it as stated in a letter to me from the Rev. D. Platt, for nine years one of its pastors. "A mutual council had been called to settle some difficulties between the pastor and some of his people. On assembling, a file of papers was presented, containing certain charges against the pastor, Rev. Mr. Walker. He declared that this was irregular, as he had not been duly notified, nor had the proper steps been taken in private with him; and, moreover, he said he was a member of the presbytery and could only be tried by that body. The council decided that they could not do anything ecclesiastically in the case. A dead silence then followed of long and painful duration. The church was in a fearful dilemma. No one could imagine what the consequences might be if the matter should be left in that position. To all human appearance, the church must be rent in twain, if not totally ruined, by a protracted controversy. At length, Mr. Lansing, of Auburn (he was not then a D. D.), stood up, and pulling off his greatcoat very deliberately said: 'Though we have nothing to do as an ecclesiastical council, we have something to do as Christian brethren, to save this church from distraction, and save the souls of the people in this place from being ruined by the quarrels of church-members.' He then proceeded, in strains of burning eloquence, to show what would be

the effect on the destiny of immortal souls, of
the continuance of this quarrel in the church;
and made an appeal to the disaffected brethren, which all who ever heard the man can
well imagine must have been irresistible. He
was followed by other members of the council,
who, in words of pathetic tenderness, urged
the settlement of the difficulty *by mutual confession and mutual forgiveness.*   And then
they united in earnest prayer for the Spirit of
God to move on the hearts of these brethren,
and bring them together.   The Spirit was
manifestly present; all were tenderly affected,
and many were in tears.   Mr. Walker made
a few remarks, indicating a kind and forgiv-
ing spirit, and making such confessions as a
good man may always make, without admit-
ting at all the charges preferred against him.

" His accusers were *pricked in their hearts,*
and began to confess, each for himself, that
he was wrong, and to take back all that he
had said against the pastor.   Finally, the
principal accuser (I knew him well; he was
a good man, though very impulsive and head-
strong at times) came forward, and put all his
papers in the fire; then fell on his knees
before his injured pastor, and begged his forgiveness, acknowledging that he had slan-

dered and abused him without any just cause or provocation. The friends of Mr. Walker now began to feel twinges of conscience. So they began to make confessions, and to ask forgiveness, till finally there was not a member of the church but had some confession to make for himself, and some word of kindness and forgiveness towards his erring brethren.

"Thus the work went on for several hours. Meantime, the people outside were waiting to be called in to hear the results. It was growing late in the afternoon. In their anxiety, two or three volunteered to go into the upper room, where the council sat, promising to come back and report, but they did not come. And finally the whole company were crowded into that little chamber, awestruck and spellbound at what they saw and heard. The meeting was continued through the whole afternoon, and far into the evening, and ended in the complete settlement of all their difficulties, and the united action of the church in labors and prayers for a revival. Indeed, there was a revival already commenced, both in the church and out of it. Many careless sinners who went into the room to see what was going on among Christians went home to weep and pray for themselves. A work of grace, the fruits of which were felt for a whole generation, had its commencement in the efforts of that council to settle difficulties by inducing mutual confession and mutual forgiveness. Mr. Walker prosecuted his labors with renewed energy and with great success, having the hearts of all the people with him; but in the midst of his work he was called to his rest, leaving others to gather in the harvest.

"I believe the church in Homer has never since had occasion to call a council for any such purpose. The remembrance of this one council and its results has always sufficed to direct the labors of pastors and brethren, and bring the church together again, even when sorely tried by internal dissensions."

This is an illustration of the excellency of the Congregational plan for mutual councils for *advice*. The parties calling this one all supposed it could act by authority, but in the absence of power accomplished the desired end by *advice* and prayer.

In 1804 the church was connected with the Middle Association, but in 1808 it connected itself with the Albany Presbyterian Synod, on the old plan of union. But soon after I became its pastor the General Assembly of the Presbyterian church passed an ordinance requiring all such churches to *perfect their organization* by electing ruling elders, and becoming, in fact, Presbyterian. To this, the Homer church, and some others like it, demurred and withdrew from presbytery and united with associations soon after formed, that with which the Homer church connected itself being the Central, covering the ground from Syracuse on the north to Broome county on the south, and the vicinity on each side. This was the beginning of a movement which materially changed the ecclesiastical aspect of the interior of the state, and gave a new impulse to Congregationalism, making the denomination an independent body.

During my pastorate at Homer I was called to another important service, one of the most important of my life. It was about the close of the War of the Rebellion, during which some three million slaves in the Southern states had been emancipated. The American Missionary Association, in New York, had entered upon its great work of educating and evangelizing this vast body of freedmen, and had sent two agents to England to solicit pecuniary aid in its work, and there was developed there much interest in behalf of the

freedmen.   Those who had been laboring in
England for the Association were about to
discontinue the work, and I was solicited, by
the Association, to represent it there, and continue it.   They asked my church to grant me
leave of absence for several months to undertake the mission.   The request was granted,
and I was quite willing to enter upon it,
partly because of my great interest in the
freedmen's cause, and partly because it would
enable me to see the Old World.

CHAPTER XXII

I at once made arrangements to enter upon the work, and proceeded to New York, where I received my commission and instructions. After a pleasant passage by steamer I arrived in Liverpool, and, after a short excursion with a family belonging to my church to Warwick Castle and Kenilworth, I hastened to Bristol, where the Congregational Union of England and Wales was to meet, and was entertained by the United States consul, whom I had known in Chicago as a member of the First Church, and an earnest anti-slavery man. There I spoke for the first time at a freedmen's meeting, and had an opportunity to witness the English mode of conducting public meetings, and also to attend the sessions of the Congregational Union.

From Bristol I went to London to report

myself to the Freedmen's Aid Society, which was coöperating with our American Missionary Association, which I was to represent.

I found the Quakers, or Friends, in England were heartily engaged in the freedmen's work, led by two prominent men of that denomination, in Birmingham, with whom I was afterwards associated for a time. I was duly recognized, and commissioned to operate under the auspices of the Freedmen's Aid Society, and arrangements were speedily made for me to begin work. At first, I was with the two Quaker gentlemen already mentioned. They had a secretary, a Baptist minister, who was to arrange for meetings, and introduce me where they were to be held. I was to have no responsibility, except to address the meetings and advocate the cause of the freedmen. It was the custom, I found, to engage some nobleman or other prominent man to preside as chairman, and nothing could be done without some such individual to sanction and give importance to the gathering.

I had no appointment to speak on my first Sabbath in London, but it was a busy day for me. In the forenoon I attended Mr. Spurgeon's service in his chapel, and after it was invited into his study for a brief conference. In the afternoon I heard Dean Stanley's funeral discourse, in Westminster Abbey, on the premier, Lord Palmerston, who had just died. In the evening I heard the celebrated Dr. Cummings preach.

Perhaps I can give no better idea of my work, while engaged in my mission to Great Britain, than by making extracts from letters written to my wife, which, fortunately, were carefully preserved by her, and are now before me. These letters formed an itinerary of my movements. I also wrote quite a number of letters to the New York *Independent*, the Boston *Congregationalist*, and a series to the *Boston Recorder*, all of which were published. The editor of the *Recorder* wrote me that those to his paper were highly appreciated.

LONDON, Nov. 1, 1865.

Dr. H. M. Storrs, who has been speaking for the freedmen, goes home on Saturday, and Mr. Martin, who has also done so, will follow the next week, and so I shall be the only American at work for the freedmen, except, perhaps, Rev. Mr. Channing, of Boston, who may speak a few times. I have been very busy during the week with the Freedmen's Aid Society, but it is slow doing anything here, they are so formal. I expect to begin active operations next week, and then I shall find enough to do. While waiting here, I have been seeing some of the sights of the great city; have passed through the tunnel under the Thames; visited the Tower, the Exchange, the Bank of England, one of the vast breweries, where there will be on hand in the spring *twelve million* gallons of porter and ale, and have been to St. James and Hyde parks, and the Billingsgate market. To-day I go to the Parliament House and Westminster Abbey. Last night I received a ticket to a grand supper in the Mansion House, for the Lord Mayor, and attended.

NEWPORT, WALES, Nov. 12.

The first series of meetings for me to attend was arranged for in South Wales, beginning at Hereford on the border. There I saw the first of the great cathedrals, after St. Paul's in London. It is a grand edifice, and has the finest altar scene in Great Britain, and some of the statuary is superior. We had an afternoon and evening meeting for the freedmen, at both of which I spoke, and much sympathy was manifested, and £250 were raised.

Lord Gage and Seal, the dean, and others of the clergy contributed. The vicar of St. Peter's presided in the evening, and made a good speech. The next day we came to Newport, and had a successful meeting, the mayor in the chair. Then we penetrated South Wales to the considerable town of Neath, where we had a still more successful meeting. The next was at Swansea. Returning to Newport, I preached here twice, to full houses, on the Sabbath, for the freedmen. We find the people very kind and hospitable, and the Friends especially interested. The scenery of the region is very fine. I felt quite at home in the pulpit on the Sabbath, the services being like our own, except that a deacon sat under the pulpit and gave out the hymns and notices.

As there was to be no meeting Monday evening, I spent the day most delightfully in sight-seeing, with a lady friend. It would astonish you to see how English ladies can walk and climb stiles. Walking three miles, we reached Caerleon, a large village, once the metropolis of Wales, and second only to London in importance. It was a walled city, several miles in circumference. Here King Arthur had his " Round Table," and this was

the scene of Tennyson's " Idylls of the King."
In the museum is a book for recording visitors'
names, and there I saw Tennyson's auto-
graph, dated 1856. I stood on the very
mound where he represents the queen as
standing, looking out for the hunters. On a
high eminence near stands an old church,
built in 1113, and from the top of the tower
there is a glorious view.

Sixteen miles distant is the Caerphilly
Castle, said to have been the largest in Great
Britain. The walls were three miles in
circumference, and the castle of immense
strength. There was a round tower at each
angle, and there is now a veritable leaning
tower of great height, inclining eleven feet
from the perpendicular. The grand hall was
seventy feet by forty, and seventeen high,
with two noble long windows, and a fireplace
nine feet wide. The date of it is lost in the
uncertainties of the past. I wandered about
in its towers and vaulted passages, and
through its open area till I was wearied and
almost lost. In a museum is a fine collection
of Roman antiquities, which have been excavated—coins in good preservation, of various
dates, from A. D. 55 to 300, vases, urns, im-
plements, lamps, earrings, studs, buckles,

statues, and memorial stones whose inscriptions are still legible. Returning here (Newport) I found, on retiring for the night, that I was almost too tired and excited by the scenes of the day to sleep.

The next morning I again took the rail in another direction, sixteen miles to Chepstow, for sixteen pence, for a visit to the far-famed Tintern Abbey. Reaching Chepstow, we took a cab and rode up the romantic valley or gorge through which flows the Wye, passing the Chepstow castle, crowning a high cliff near the town, and Wind Cliff, an elevation of nine hundred feet, from which is a view that extends to nine counties. After a ride of five miles, we came in sight of the ruins of the Abbey. They are situated immediately on the bank of the Wye, a high bluff rising precipitously from the opposite shore, while a beautiful meadow skirts the river on the side on which the Abbey stands. Nothing can surpass the picturesqueness of the first sight of the ruins, but you get no just conception of their extent until the front door is opened, and you gaze in and are filled with admiration and astonishment. It was, apparently, as large as Westminster Abbey, and even more magnificent as a work of art.

The columns, arches and windows are in a good state of preservation, and are exquisite in their construction. Heavy masses of ivy hang on the walls, and the jackdaws almost craze you with their chatterings. You ascend a flight of stone steps and walk along the walls and look down nearly one hundred feet into the interior, and are amazed at its vast extent and height. Behind it are the cloisters, the refectory, the sacristy and the hospice. The architecture is pure Gothic. It was founded in 1131 for Cistercian monks. How great must have been their number to have required such a place of worship and residence! The following extract is truthful, as I can testify:

Its pointed arches of fairy lightness, covered with ivy, rising in the centre of a sylvan valley, with the classic Wye wending its course by its side, is a sight which strikes the beholder with amazement. On entering the sacred edifice, a sudden awe thrills through the mind at the solemn stillness which pervades the place.

> Relic of by-gone days and noble arts,
> Despoiled, yet perfect, within thy circle spreads
> A holiness appealing to all hearts.

Monkish tombstones and mutilated figures are deposited about the walls. The old keeper, on learning that I was an American, said that great numbers of my countrymen had visited the Abbey, and among the rest he remembered Daniel Webster particularly. I wish I could convey some idea of the over-whelming beauty of this picturesque ruin, unsurpassed in the kingdom, but I cannot. I have secured a series of stereoscopic views which will afford my friends on my return home some faint idea of this striking and beautiful object.

MERTHYR-TYDVIL, WALES.

At this place I addressed a freedmen's meeting, and am beginning to get accustomed to the habits of the people, and their mode of conducting such assemblies. I am told that my addresses are impressive, and certainly they are well received and liberally re-sponded to. I speak to-night at Aberdare, and to-morrow evening at Abergavenny. I am meeting with good success, and certainly am enjoying myself hugely.

Few Americans visit this region of Wales, which is rich in castles, and was the last stronghold of the ancient Britons, who were conquered by the Romans. Cromwell also once fought in this part of Wales. I enjoy uncommon advantages for seeing the scenery and objects of interest, as well as the people.

The scenery of Wales is, as you know, very fine. On one of the railways, I passed through a tunnel, two and a half miles long, through the mountain, from one valley to another, and on another road I crossed a viaduct two hundred and ten feet high, from the summit of one mountain to another, and of great length. It was fearful to look down from the train upon a town below, in whose streets men seemed like pigmies.

The Welsh are a very religious people, and churches and chapels abound everywhere. The latter are occupied by dissenters, who far outnumber the churchmen. The Congregationalists, or, as they are called in Great Britain, the Independents, I am told, are the most numerous here, although there are many Baptists and Methodists. At one meeting we had a fine specimen of Welsh fire and eloquence on the part of an Independent minister, who spoke in Welsh. I find everywhere, in all denominations, a deep interest manifested for our emancipated negroes, and a readiness to contribute for their relief and improvement. We usually have both clergymen and ministers on the platform, and often one of the former presides. The Friends, or Quakers, are very zealous. From here I shall return to Birmingham, where they are to give me a formal reception at a tea-meeting, in the English style.

CHAPTER XXIII

BIRMINGHAM, Nov. 20.

The Aid Society here has voted to remit to
New York £500, which, as exchange is now
very high, will be equivalent to $2,750 there
as part of the avails· of my meetings in
Wales. So you see I am not running our Association into debt! Last evening I attended
a religious meeting of Friends in their chapel
(the first I ever was present at) to see how
they conduct one. All sat perfectly still for
nearly three quarters of an hour, and then a
man rose and said a few words; silence followed for a time, then another spoke, and
silence again prevailed; at length, after an
hour and a half, the meeting broke up.
There was no reading or singing.

The next evening I attended the tea-meeting that had been arranged for me, at the
house of a wealthy Friend, the treasurer of
the Aid Society. Invitations had been sent

to gentlemen of influence, to meet and hear from me. I spoke at length of our American affairs, and especially of the condition and needs of the freedmen. They organized with Mr. E. Sturge, brother of the celebrated philanthropist, Joseph Sturge, in the chair. After my address a very complimentary resolution was passed, expressing satisfaction at hearing from me, and commending my mission. The next day I met the Committee of the Society, and after a conference, I received their endorsement. From here I go to Manchester.

There is a great and growing interest manifested in Great Britain in behalf of the freed negroes of America, and very much has been done already for their relief and their social and religious improvement. The movement began in Birmingham, where there has been for forty years or more a very efficient anti-slavery society of ladies. At one of their meetings a year ago or more, it was suggested that something ought to be done for the freedmen of America, and it was proposed that supplies should be sent. From this resulted the very energetic Birmingham and Midland Freedmen's Aid Society, which has done so much, and which has always maintained a leading position in the efforts of British Christians and philanthropists in this direction. In this good work there, and in fact throughout England, the Friends or Quakers have borne a most honorable and noble part. It has been my good fortune to see much of this benevolent class, to experience their hospitality and to coöperate with them. And the recollection of my intercourse with them will be among the pleasantest of the reminiscences of my visit to this country.

As a specimen of the spirit that prevails at Birmingham, I will state that some time ago they had a public breakfast there for the benefit of the freedmen's cause. Mr. John Cropper of Liverpool, a most liberal and benevolent man, not a Quaker, however, offered a donation of £50 if £1,000 could be raised. The effort was made, and resulted in securing £1,200 or about $6,000. Large amounts of clothing have also been sent from that society. The London Freedmen's Aid Society is also another very efficient organization, and the Friends' Central Committee of London another. But besides these three leading associations there are some forty or fifty local ones in various parts of the kingdom. There has been, also, a National

Committee of British Freedmen's Aid Societies at London, of which Sir T. Fowell Buxton is chairman, designed to be a sort of bond of union for all the local societies.

This last named committee held its third quarterly meeting in Manchester, where I now write, this week, and arrangements were inaugurated, which will be carried out, for making of this committee a National Union of Freedmen's Aid Societies for Great Britain and Ireland. To this central body reports will be made, and through it arrangements carried out for the more general and efficient prosecution of the work of raising funds for the freedmen of America.

In connection with the business meeting of the National Committee here, a public meeting was held after the English manner, with speeches, contributions, etc. In the evening a more popular gathering was had with addresses. I was invited to be present and to speak, which I did. There were subscribed at both meetings £500 or $2,500, of which a part was voted to be sent to the American Missionary Association, which I represent.

While in Birmingham I received an invitation to hold a freedmen's meeting at Kendal, the southern entrance to the celebrated lake region, famous as the residence of the lake poets and other literary persons. The meeting at Kendal was well attended and satisfactory in pecuniary returns. Leaving there I passed up through the lake country.

CHAPTER XXIV

Leaving Kendal by rail at 6:30 o'clock,
A. M., I was soon set down at the Windermere hotel, nine miles distant, in the village
of the same name near the shore of the lake.
After an excellent breakfast, I walked out
among the many beautiful parks which are
connected with the country seats that abound
here, and in the course of my stroll passed
the house, Elleray, where Christopher North
(Professor Wilson) of Blackwood fame, spent
so much of his time. It is a plain dwelling,
but delightfully situated on high ground, commanding a view of the lake and much of the
immediately surrounding country. After satisfying my curiosity here, and purchasing
some fine pictures of the scenery of the
district, I took a gig and driver and set off
for Grasmere, after riding about a little to
get some lake views, and to obtain sight of

some more of the beautiful residences of the neighborhood.

Going north, we skirted Windermere lake, getting many fine views, and ere long came in sight of " Dove's Nest," the residence of the late Mrs. Hemans. On reaching the village of Ambleside, I was pointed to the house where Harriet Martineau now lives. She is very aged, and has not been out for four or five years. A little farther on upon a hillside, peeping out of the woods, we saw where Dr. Arnold lived. At the village of Rydal we halted, while I ran up the ravine to catch a look at a waterfall which is much admired, but of which we have thousands in the United States quite as fine, and so common as to be thought little of. In fact, I saw no cascade in the district which would be celebrated in America, though here they excite great admiration.

Just beyond Rydal village, and near the roadside, is Rydal Mount, where Wordsworth lived and died. It is not a pretentious house, but stands on elevated ground and is surrounded by shrubbery, and in front has a small grass plat with seats, from which there is a fine outlook down the valley. Here the poet used often to sit. I obtained entrance to

the grounds but not to the dwelling. Rydal
Water is a beautiful little sheet, very shallow,
and filled with green islands—what we
should call a pond in America.

By the roadside and just in the edge of the
water rises a high rock which is ascended by
steps and on which I was told Wordsworth
used to sit for hours, in fine weather, reading,
or writing poetry. Near by, and on. the side
of the road, is a very common house, now
used for some kind of a shop, in part, where
S. T. Coleridge lived for a while. There also
dwelt Hartley Coleridge, and there he died.

Two or three miles further brought me to
Grasmere, village and lake, where I visited
the quaint little church in which the Words-
worths worshiped, and which contains a plain
marble slab with a memorial inscription for
the poet. In the burying-ground surrounding
the church, and in the corner nearly behind
it, I found the graves of Wordsworth and his
sister, with Miss Hutchinson's, his wife's
maiden sister, between. They are all marked
by plain marble stones. Behind them lies
Hartley Coleridge. In the village is pointed
out the humble cottage where Wordsworth
first lived, before the house at Rydal Mount
was built.

At Grasmere I dismissed my horse and driver and after a lunch at the hotel I resolved to occupy the afternoon with a pedestrian trip, leaving my luggage to come on by coach. Proceeding on then, over the fine macadamized road, I had an excellent opportunity to enjoy the scenery, albeit the season was not the most favorable for the purpose, nor the day propitious. It had been cloudy since morning, and a mist which occasionally rose hung over the valley. But just as I left Grasmere the sun broke through the clouds and I had some glorious views, particularly one of the high mountain peak on the top of which are seen, quite distinctly, two rocks which remarkably resemble a lion and a lamb. The valley varies from half a mile to a mile in width, and the mountains rise to a very considerable height, bare for the most part of trees, and resembling those in many parts of California.

I sauntered on leisurely, intending to make about five miles by dark, and to reach a roadside inn where I had directed the Keswick coach to take me up. But so excellent was the road and so exciting my experience, that when I arrived at my appointed goal there was more than an hour of daylight left and I felt so fresh that I concluded to push on to another inn three miles farther. The road was not level, but up hill and down, and often did I stop to look behind me or to gaze on some new scene before. For a large portion of the last stage my course was along a lake, the name of which I have forgotten, and under the lofty peak called Helvellyn, which towers above all the others in the valley and rises directly from the water's edge.

Nothing strikes an American more than the excellence of these roads. They are all macadamized and kept as smooth and clean as Beacon Street in Boston, multitudes of poor people earning a small pittance to eke out their little means of subsistence by gathering up the scrapings in wheelbarrows or carts drawn by a scrubby little pony or a shaggy donkey.

In one place, as I walked on, I discovered a flat stone set in the wall fence, with an inscription cut upon it, which I supposed was a memorial of some person killed by accident there. I have seen monuments of the kind by the roadside in America. But on examination I found it to relate to a *horse*, and I copied it as follows :

30th 9th mo. 1843.

> Fall'n from his fellow's side
> The steed beneath is lying;
> In harness here he died;
> His only fault was—dying.

W. B.

At length I reached " mine inn," just as the darkness was settling down upon the valley, and sat down before a blazing coal fire to wait for the coach, improving the time by getting a cup of tea *with cream*, a plate of toast, and a fresh boiled egg. At seven o'clock the coach came rattling on at the rate of seven or eight miles an hour and took me up, and before nine we were in Keswick.

As I must take the train about noon the next day, I rose early and had my breakfast just as the day was dawning, and then mounted a spirited little pony, which I had engaged the night before, for a ride round Lake Derwentwater, a distance of about ten miles. The morning was delightful, clear and balmy, and never did I find my spirits more exhilarated than during that trip. The scenery of Keswick and its lake is equal to any thing I have ever seen, and I have visited most of the celebrated regions of the Eastern and Middle States and California.

The lake is some four or five miles long and from half a mile to two miles wide in different parts, and lies in a basin formed by bare and precipitous mountains that rise almost from its edge, but endlessly variegated in ·form and appearance. On the route I paused to look at two cascades that attracted much attention, one whose name, Lodore, has become so familiar from Southey's lines written for his son and entitled " How the Waters come down at Lodore." ·But neither of these would excite much observation in America.

On an island in the lake is a large mansion belonging to Lord Derwentwater, and there are several fine mansions on either side overlooking the water. On my return, just before reaching Keswick town, a place of several thousand inhabitants, I came upon the old church where Southey attended service. Part of it dates back six hundred years, and there is a fine marble statue of the poet, in a recumbent position, the face formed from a cast taken some years before his death and said to be a good likeness. The old sexton (claiming to be the oldest in England) was full of anecdotes of Southey, who, he said, " was a very humble man," and of Southey's house, Greta Hall, occupied by him for forty years, fronting the lake. This lake region is one of the most attractive to the tourist of any in England.

CHAPTER XXV

AYR, SCOTLAND, Dec. 27, 1865.

Coming north from Liverpool one passes Carlisle, a large town, the last of importance in England, and soon crosses a little streamlet, that he might easily leap over, which forms the boundary line between the two kingdoms. Then he reaches Gretna Green, and the house and shop of the blacksmith who used to forge the chains of matrimony for runaways from the strict laws of England to the looser ones of Scotland. A little further on he reaches Dumfries, where the poet Burns lived a while and acted as exciseman, and where he finally died and was buried. Still further on is Mauchline, near which was the farm of Mossgiel, where much of his poetry was written.

I reached Ayr, where he was born, in the evening, and took lodgings at the Queen's Hotel, which fronts on the river Ayr, and a few rods from the " Brig of Ayr," that is, the bridge, in Scottish. Who does not remember the lines on " The Twa Brigs of Ayr," immortalized by the peasant poet? I could not delay visiting them, with a friend residing here, night though it was, as soon as I had deposited my baggage and engaged a room. I crossed the " auld brig," and returned by the new. The former is very ancient, built in the reign of Alexander III, about 1250. It is very narrow and well deserved the taunt of the " new brig " for being so narrow that two wheelbarrows could scarcely pass each other upon it. It is now used only by foot passengers.

Below the brigs and near the mouth of the river are the remains of a fort built by Cromwell in 1652. There are some 18,000 people now in the town. Here Wallace was once confined in a tower, and he and Bruce once figured largely in the vicinity, as you know. Not far from here the latter landed, and the scene occurred where he saw the spider who encouraged him by her repeated efforts, as he lay disheartened in a cave just before the decisive battle of Bannockburn, where the English were defeated and Scotland's independence was won.

There is a peculiar interest connected with any place associated with the memory of such a man as Burns. I cannot describe my emotions as I thought of being on a spot of which I had so often read, and as I sat down in the room at the hotel with a copy of the life and writings of the poet, and perused them till near midnight, refreshing my recollections of his history and his works, and in the morning set off for a walk to the cottage in which he was born, about two miles distant, near which, also, was the scene of Tam O'Shanter's adventures. In passing through one of the principal streets, I saw the sign of the " Tam O'Shanter Inn," on which was a notice that cup and chairs used by Tam and Souter John are still preserved within. A very good painting over the door represents Tam just setting off on his mare Maggie on his famous trip, the landlord and his wife, and Souter John bidding him good night, a lantern flashing its light on the scene.

After a pleasant walk over a fine road and in view of several beautiful mansions, I reached the cottage, now owned and preserved by an · association of shoemakers. There are seen the little room in which Burns was born, with the recess for the bed, the stone floor, and the little solitary window with four diminutive panes of glass, and the large fireplace. Adjoining this room is another small one with chairs, tables, etc., as in his days of infancy, and these are literally covered with names and initials carved by fools who vainly hoped thus to link their names with immortality along with Burns. A little farther on are the walls of "Auld Alloway Kirk," where Tam O'Shanter saw the hobgoblins and witches, and the window is pointed out through which he peered in and and saw the De'il playing the pipes for them to dance, he sitting in a recess that still appears! Here Tam spoke, when, suddenly, the lights disappeared and after him came the whole brood, while Maggie, the grey mare, put to her mettle, made for the brig across the Doon, near by, the centre of which stream the witches could not cross. We walked down the road in the track of Tam, and across the bridge, stopping opposite the keystone or centre, where Maggie lost her tail (!) to enjoy a hearty laugh at the humor of the idea.

An old man, such as is always seen hanging about such places in Europe, designated for us the various points of interest.

We saw the place where the thorn stood on which

> Mungo's mither hang'd hersel';

also

> The ford,
> Whare in the snaw the chapman smoor'd;

and the

> Meikle stane,
> Whare drunken Charlie brak 's neck-bane;

as well as

> The cairn,
> Whare hunters fand the murder'd bairn.

How descriptive of the condition of one under the influence of liquor, those lines

> Kings may be blest, but Tam was glorious,
> O'er a' the ills o' life victorious.

In front of "Auld Alloway Kirk" is the grave of Burns' father and mother, marked by the same headstone, and across the road stands the new and handsome Alloway church. A few rods from the latter, in an enclosure ornamented with shrubs and flowers, and laid out with walks, stands a handsome monument to the poet, supposed to be on the identical spot on which he wrote the exquisite little song beginning

> Ye banks and braes o' bonnie Doon,
> How can ye bloom sae fresh and fair!

The Doon is a beautiful stream, and well deserves the poet's praises, with its picturesque shores and distant hillsides.   In a little building, also standing in the enclosure referred to, is a most capital piece of statuary, representing Tam O'Shanter and Souter John in the tavern, the latter just reaching the point of one of his funny stories, and Tam shaking his sides with laughter.   The attitudes and the expressions of the countenances are equal to anything I have ever seen, although the artist was self-taught.

After enjoying these scenes I returned to my lodgings by another road, from which I obtained a view of the sea, of a remarkable promontory that projects into it, and of the ruins of an old castle,—to reflect on the sad fact that talents like those of Burns should be associated with such morals as his.   But immoral as he was, we cannot but admire his genius and read his poems and songs, while we lament that religion did not exert her purifying influence over his heart.   One redeeming quality he certainly had, which it were well if others of sterner morals developed as fully—he was kind-hearted and benevolent.   It is related of him that when in most straitened circumstances pecuniarily, his hand was open to the needy. The wandering poor were never allowed to go past his door without a halfpenny or a handful of meal. He was particularly kind to those who were weak in mind. A poor half-mad creature, the Madge Wildfire of Scott, it is said, always found a mouthful ready for her at his fireside. It is also asserted that he never was so addicted to drink as to neglect his official duties, and that he superintended the education of his family with great care, and especially that of his eldest son. He was a great republican in politics, and once when a toast was given to Pitt where he was present, he refused to drink it, and proposed instead of it, that of " a better man, Washington." Never did I enjoy the poems of Burns as when reading them in his own town.

From Ayr I went to Irvine, a few miles distant, where I preached twice on the Sabbath for the freedmen. I was the guest of the eccentric but able United Presbyterian minister, Rev. W. H. Robertson, whom I shall long remember. This was the birthplace of James Montgomery, the poet, and the little thatched cottage in which he was born now stands under the same roof with what was then the Moravian chapel. I visited it in a little lane or close. How different the character and writings of the two poets, and how remarkable that two such geniuses should arise so near together in such humble homes! Kilmarnock, near by, where I am to speak to-morrow, was the birthplace of Alexander Smith, also a poet. One is continually coming here upon places memorable for something in history or literature with which he is familiar.

I next visited Paisley, a town of some thirty thousand people, famous for its shawls and the great Coats establishment for the manufacture of spool cotton. Mr. Peter Coats showed me through his immense factory, and presented me with a package of his spool thread, so well known in America. I saw immense piles of the peculiar wood which is alone adapted to his use for spools. Mr. Coats is a warm-hearted and liberal man, and took a deep interest in my mission.

Paisley owes its origin to a religious establishment founded here in 1160 by Warner Stuart, ancestor of the royal family of Scotland and of Queen Victoria. The present abbey church belongs to the present established body, and is a great curiosity. The portion now used for public worship consists of the old chancel, and there is a very fine Gothic window. Two noble families have seats there, and several have vaults in the cemetery. A crypt on one side has a remarkable echo, and within it is a recumbent statue of Marjory, daughter of Robert Bruce, who was buried there. She was the mother of Robert II, and wife of the founder of the abbey. In the graveyard was pointed out where Burns' "Bonny Lass of Ballochmoyle" lies interred.

I preached three times on Sunday in Paisley, in three different churches, the Free, the United Presbyterian, and the Established. In the latter case, for the first time, I wore the gown and bands, as without them I could not be permitted to occupy the pulpit, and there, too, for the first time, I heard sung the old Scotch version of the Psalms. Before entering the pulpit the sexton arrayed me in the gown and bands, and with some difficulty I ascended the pulpit stairs, nearly tripping with the gown. I was the guest of the United Presbyterian minister, and his wife told me afterwards, "You looked fine in the gown!" Much sympathy was manifested in all the congregations for the freedmen, and good collections were taken.

CHAPTER XXVI

My next field of effort in my mission was at
Edinburgh, and I was exceedingly desirous of
making a demonstration there that would open
the way for operations in the interior of Scotland. The freedmen's cause had never been
presented there. I succeeded in securing the
pulpits of three churches to present the subject—the Free High Church, Dr. Arnot's,
the Congregational, Dr. Lindsay Alexander's, and for the evening, the immense Free
Church Assembly Hall, where there was a
crowded audience.

I called on the celebrated Dr. Guthrie,
and was invited to breakfast with him; he
manifested great interest in my mission, and
was very desirous of having a public week-
evening meeting, with the lord provost to preside. He had, himself, been forbidden for
some time, by his physician, to speak in public, but I very much wished to have him do
so in this case, on account of his great elo-

quence and popularity. He finally consented to consult his medical adviser, and after a careful examination the doctor said, " Loose him and let him go," and so his aid was secured.

After much travel and effort a large hall was secured, the services of the lord provost engaged, and public announcements were made. I found it a no small undertaking to accomplish this in such a city. When the evening came the house was full, and on reaching the place I found quite a number of prominent persons, including Dr. Guthrie and the provost, awaiting me in the ante-room. At eight o'clock we entered the crowded room in solemn procession, led by the provost, who made a short opening speech. After I had set forth as well as I could and at length the object of my mission, Dr. Alexander moved a resolution of sympathy, with a good speech. He was seconded by Dr. Arnot, and it was adopted. Then a gentleman moved the formation of a committee for raising subscriptions outside, which was followed by his heading the list with £200, or $1,000. At once £500 were added, or $2,500, and subsequently it was increased by considerable additions. Then Rev. Dr. Guthrie rose to move a vote of thanks to the gentleman from America, for the information given, and supported it for half an hour in a most capital and characteristic address, replete with pathos and humor in parts, which was loudly cheered. He expressed much sympathy for America in her great work, and for the freedmen in their new condition. He said no other cause would have brought him out. He is still nominally pastor of a church with Dr. Hanna, but does not discharge any of the duties of the office. I found him very genial and entertaining. The meeting proved to be quite a success, much to my relief and that of some timid friends, and it will have great influence in Scotland. I think the total receipts of my operations there were over five thousand dollars. It was a great feat to get up and "get off" such a meeting in that city.

On calling on Mr. Arnot at Morningside, a suburb of Edinburgh, I was shown by him into Dr. Chalmers's study, which remains just as he left it, books, pictures, desk, chairs, etc. Mr. Arnot occupies the house and by the lease this room was stipulated to be left as it is. It was with deep emotion that I stood in that room and thought of the gigantic labors of its former occupant. In the cemetery near by I also saw Dr. Chalmers's tomb and the stone that marks his resting-place, and near by that of Hugh Miller. Dr. Guthrie is also to be buried there.

My mission, I repeat, has given me unequalled opportunities for seeing scenery and objects of interest, and much that escapes the mere tourist. In fact, my work led me to all parts of England and Scotland, almost from Land's End to John O'Groat's. While in Edinburgh I made an excursion to Melrose Abbey. But it has been so often described that I will not dwell upon it, only to say that it is, next to Tintern, the finest specimen of Gothic architecture in Great Britain. The eastern window is uncommonly elegant, and as Scott says in the "Lay of the Last Minstrel," as if

> Some fairy's hand
> 'Twixt poplars straight the ozier's wand
> In many a freaking knot had twined;
> Then framed a spell when work was done,
> And changed the willow wreaths to stone.

Here the embalmed heart of Robert the Bruce was finally deposited.

A ride of three miles through a romantic region brought me to the former residence of

Sir Walter Scott, who has been my favorite novelist from my youth up. It has often been described and I will only say that the edifice, so unlike any other ever built, is well worth seeing, and is as full of curiosities as was Barnum's museum. Says Elihu Burritt:

And here it is! It is the photograph of Sir Walter, and brimful of him and his histories. No author's pen ever gave such individuality to a human home. . . . History hangs its web-work everywhere. Quaint, old, carved stones from abbey and castle ruins, arms, devices and inscriptions are all here presented to the eye like the printed page of an open volume. Here is a chair made from the house in which Wallace was betrayed, Rob Roy's pistol, and the key and door of the old Tolbooth of Edinburgh.

It is with the deepest emotion that one enters the dwelling so associated with the Great Wizard of the North, whose enchantment he has completely experienced. As I walked from room to room, saw the furniture, the presents received from Napoleon and other royal personages, and looked from the windows out upon the scenes familiar to Sir Walter, I could not but feel sad that "the places he knew would know him no more." But my feelings culminated almost to tears when I entered the study, kept just as he left it, and saw the books he consulted, the arm-chair he occupied, and the desk on which he wrote his immortal works, which have afforded me and thousands of others so much entertainment. But what shall I say of the emotion felt when, in a little glass case I looked upon the very clothes he wore when he walked out upon his grounds! Here was the white hat he used to be pictured in, the thick shoes, the coat and plaid trowsers in which he loved to be clad. After examining these things, I took a stroll about the grounds, and down to the Tweed, and thought how often Scott had trod these paths, and I meditated on the lessons here suggested of the muta-bility of life. The library is an immense room and contains some twenty thousand volumes. But I need not enlarge. That evening I returned to Edinburgh after a day of excitement and interest rarely equaled in my experience.

CHAPTER XXVII

I had a letter of introduction from President
Sturtevant of Illinois College to James Douglas, Esq., of Cavers, near Hawick, about
fifty miles southeast of Edinburgh, and this
secured for me an invitation to spend a few
days with him at his residence, and also to
address a public meeting, at which he presided, in behalf of the American freedmen.
Hawick, now a flourishing manufacturing
town of some eight thousand inhabitants, on
the Teviot, "was a rallying and sallying
point in the old border wars, and was inun-
dated two or three times by the flux and reflux
of this conflict." It suffered much in those
days when freebooting was the pastime and
occupation of knights and chieftains and their
clans, being in the border country of Scotland
adjoining that of Northumberland in England, the home of the Percys.

On my arrival in Hawick, I was first set down by the omnibus at the Tower Hotel, a building that was once the grand mansion of the noble house of Buccleuch, and where, as has been said, the Duchess of Monmouth used to hold her drawing-rooms in an apartment which many a New England journeyman mechanic would hardly think ample and comfortable enough for his parlor. Our freedmen's meeting was held in a large United Presbyterian church in Hawick. Much interest was manifested in the object, and a committee was appointed to solicit subscriptions, the head of which was Mr. Douglas on the part of the gentlemen, and his excellent wife on the part of the ladies, Mr. Douglas also heading the list of donors.

Mr. Douglas is the son of James Douglas, Esq., of Cavers, who is well known in the literary and religious world as a great philanthropist and the author of several works which have had a high reputation, " The Advancement of Society," " Errors in Religion," " Thoughts on Missions," etc. He was a laird of extensive estates, and yet a decided and intelligent Congregationalist, as is also the present Mr. Douglas, who though not a publicist, in other respects follows in his father's footsteps, not only in philanthropic labors, but also in occasional services as a lay preacher. Mr. Douglas is descended by a younger line from the celebrated border chieftains, the earls of Douglas, the lifelong foes of the Percys. His wife is the daughter of the well-known Sir Andrew Agnew, who did so much to promote the right observance of the Sabbath. She sympathizes fully with her husband in his religious views, and coöperates with him in his plans of benevolence.

The dwelling which Mr. Douglas occupies was once a castle and has stood the brunt of war in ancient times. In some places the walls are eight or ten feet thick. It stands about three miles from Hawick, not far from the Teviotside and in full view of the Eildon Hills and ·"Minto's Crag." The estates are nearly thirteen miles long, by several wide. Near the dwelling stands an ancient, though humble, parish church, now used for a schoolhouse, in which Dr. Chalmers officiated for a time, in early life, as assistant minister, and where Boston, author of the "Fourfold State," has also preached. The place is pointed out where he used to stand on the steps sometimes, and address the crowds of people outside.

Mr. Douglas has now in his possession, carefully preserved in a box, the banner which his ancestor bore, as hereditary sheriff, five hundred years ago at the famous battle of Otterburn, or Chevy Chase, in which James, Earl of Douglas, was slain, and Percy Hotspur taken prisoner. He has also two ladies' gauntlets of the same date, elaborately worked, which, borne on a Percy's lance, a Douglas captured. Besides these interesting objects, he has also one of the original parchment copies of the "Act and Covenant" of the Scots, which his ancestor, as sheriff, had committed to him, with the signatures of the nobles, gentlemen, etc., of his district.

While visiting Mr. Douglas, he proposed that I should accompany himself and wife to the Abbey of Jedburgh, about nine miles distant. This I was but too happy to do. We accordingly set out early in the morning in a carriage, our course taking us down Teviotdale for a short distance, and thence across the hills to Jedburgh. Teviotdale is a part of the scene of Scott's "Lay of the Last Minstrel." Branksome Tower, where the chief events of the story occurred, is about three miles from Hawick, in an opposite direction to Cavers. From Branksome, Sir

William of Deloraine set out on his remarkable ride to see the magician Michael Scott
of Melrose Abbey.   This was his charge:

> Sir William of Deloraine, good at need,
> Mount thee on the wightest steed;
> Spare not to speer, nor stint to ride,
> Until thou come to fair Tweedside.

The Tweed and the Teviot unite their
waters not far from Melrose.

> And in Melrose's holy pile
> Seek thou the Monk of St. Mary's aisle.
>
> *   *   *   *   *   *   *   *
>
> Soon in his saddle sat he fast,
> And soon the steep descent he past,
> Soon cross'd the sounding barbican,
> And soon the Teviot's side he won.
>
> *   *   *   *   *   *   *   *
>
> In Hawick twinkled many a light,
> Behind him soon they set in night.
>
> *   *   *   *   *   *   *   *
>
> He turned him now from Teviot's side,
> And guided by the tinkling rill
> Northward the dark ascent did ride,
> And gained the moor at Horslie hill.
> Broad on the left before him lay
> For many a mile the Roman way.
> A moment now he slacked his speed,
> A moment breath'd his panting steed;
> Drew saddle-girth and corselet-band,
> And loosened in the sheath his brand.

> On Minto-Crags the moonbeams glint,
> Where Barnbill hewed his bed of flint,
> Who flung his outlawed limbs to rest,
> Where falcons hang their giddy nest,
> Mid cliffs from where his eagle eye
> For many a league his prey could spy.

All these points thus alluded to we saw in the course of our journey. Below us as we climbed the hills lay the beautiful Teviotdale, the river rolling between highly cultivated fields which stretched from its banks in each direction, up to and along the sides of the hills; Minto's rough crags and the point where Deloraine "drew saddle girth" and "breathed his panting steed." In the distance we saw Minto House, the seat of the Earl of Minto, and passed through Denholm village, the birthplace of Leyden the poet, where a beautiful monument has been erected to his memory on the village green. Among the inscriptions on the monument is a tribute from Sir Walter Scott, and another is an extract from his own poems, entitled, "Scenes of My Infancy," a tender appeal to the citizens of his native place to hold him in kind remembrance.

Reaching at length the village of Jedburgh, a real Scotch town of some 3,000 people, we ordered dinner at an inn and then set forth to find the Abbey. It is one of the oldest in Scotland, St. Kenoch being Abbot A. D. 1000. The place was the chief town of the middle marches, and defended by castle and numerous towers, and was often the rendez-vous of the Scotch armies. David I, that "sore saint for the crown," enlarged and richly endowed the Abbey in the twelfth century. As I have found to be the case very often, a part of the old edifice has been fitted up and used as a parish church in connection with the Presbyterian Establishment. At one time, some years ago, one of the "private chapels" was occupied for a school and there Sir David Brewster (a native of Jedburgh) was a pupil, and also the celebrated Mrs. Somerville, author of the "Connection of the Physical Sciences." Her father was parish minister, and near by stands the manse in which Mrs. Somerville was born. I think Sir David's elder brother kept the school. In it also the poet Thompson and Samuel Ruther-ford received the rudiments of their education.

Some parts of the ruins of the Abbey are still in good preservation. There is a Nor-man arch over the doorway which forms the principal entrance, which has been much admired. The workmanship is delicate and beautiful. Over the intersection of the nave and transept rises a massive square tower, with irregular turrets and belfry, 100 feet high. Considerable sums have been expended in restoring decayed parts of the building. It is greatly to the credit of the Queen that she is much interested in preserving relics of antiquity, such as these, and the Imperial government aids in some cases in the work of restoration or preservation.

In this Abbey was married Alexander III, in 1285, that monarch whose decease, being childless, gave rise to the dispute about the succession and the rival claims of Baliol and the Bruce. The spot at the high altar where the wedding ceremony took place is pointed out. The castle of Jedburgh, on an eminence not far off, was a favorite residence of the kings from David I to Alexander III, and Malcolm IV died in it.

In the lower part of the town still stands a quaint and queer old house which we visited, where Queen Mary lay sick for several weeks on a time. She rode forty miles on horseback in a single day, which threw her into a fever. It was curious to see the little pent-up rooms, the narrow stone staircases, the antiquated furniture still preserved, the tapestry bedstead, kitchen, etc., which now would be considered hardly worthy of the humblest family.

The people of Jedburgh were somewhat famous in the wars of olden time. They have still preserved a flag or pennon taken at Bannockburn.

Returning to the inn, we partook of a good dinner and then returned to Cavers, which we reached about dark, after enjoying a most delightful excursion. I found Mr. Douglas and his lady deeply interested in American affairs, and full of sympathy for the freedmen. Their hospitality was ample and I shall ever remember my few days at Cavers with pleasure. I wish there were more such lairds in Scotland. But I must add, I have nowhere been more kindly welcomed and hospitably entertained than in that country.

EDINBURGH, Jan. 8, 1866.

Leaving Cavers after a delightful visit, I returned to Edinburgh. I have none but pleasant recollections of this city, and had not so much been written about it, I should like to dwell upon its beauties and peculiarities, and the numerous objects of interest. Of course I visited the famous castle which overtowers the city, and saw the crown jewels of Scotland, went through the old palace of Holyrood, climbed to Arthur's seat, walked through the old cemetery of St. Giles and saw the beautiful and unique statue of Walter Scott, etc. I shall always remember my visit here with deep interest, the very successful freedmen's meeting held here, the acquaintance formed with the ministers, and the generous sympathy manifested by all denominations in the work of caring for and elevating our four millions of manumitted slaves.

Yesterday was my birthday, and, fortunately, having no engagement to speak, I spent the day quietly, except that I heard Dr. Hanna, the biographer of Dr. Chalmers, preach, and also Dr. Candlish, a Free Church leader. I had the evening for reflection, and found I had much cause for gratitude to God, and I made a new consecration of myself to him. I did not forget to thank him for my domestic happiness, and that he had given me such a helper in you. How appropriate were the lines of Addison :—

> God's bounteous love with earthly bliss,
> Has made my cup run o'er,
> And in a kind and faithful friend
> Has doubled all my store.

I sometimes feel homesick, especially when I get letters from you, and am almost tired of change and sightseeing, and long to be *at home*, engaged in my loved pastoral work. But I must go on and finish my mission. I think I have done some good, and I am sure I have found much pleasure. From here I go into the interior of Scotland to hold freedmen's meetings.

CHAPTER XXVIII

ALLOA, SCOTLAND.

Having arranged for a public meeting at the old and famous town of Stirling, I came here and preached on Sunday, and then went to Dunfermline, and interested the minister there, and arranged for a meeting. At this place (Alloa) on Sunday evening, a gentleman called on me with a collection worth in New York $750, and offered to go out with me the next day and call on some wealthy persons. My Sabbaths have been very fruitful pecuniarily. One gentleman who subscribed $500, paid it to me, and added $100 more for himself and a like sum for his brother. In all I received what is worth in New York, with exchange, $1,000; and more will be collected. Pretty well for one Sabbath! I am and have been very well; have not had even a cold.

I enjoyed my visit to Stirling exceedingly, and had a very successful public meeting and a liberal collection. There is no spot in Scotland more full of historic associations than this, and none, except Edinburgh, that a stranger is more delighted with. The height on which the castle, and most of the present town, now stands, rises from the midst of a vast level plain, very much as the pictures represent Athens. If the hill were swept away, the plain would resemble one of our largest Western prairies. I ascended to the castle on a beautiful clear morning. I never saw this view equaled. It is said to extend, in good weather, one hundred and twenty miles. On every side are finely cultivated meadows. In the distance are seen the Grampians, Ben Lomond, the Ochil Hills and the heights beyond Bannockburn, while the river Forth winds and twists itself up, infinitely more than the Connecticut as seen from Mt. Holyoke, and you can scarcely see an acre that has not been part of a battlefield. Unless Edinburgh be an exception, Stirling was the strongest citadel in Scotland. The field of Bannockburn, where Bruce defeated the English and secured the independence of Scotland, is in full view from the castle. On another side, at Stirling bridge, Wallace's famous battle and defeat of the English at an earlier period occurred, and just beyond is the craig on and behind which he hid his army, and on which is now erected an immense tower to his memory. In another direction was fought a battle in which James III fell. In 1304 the castle held out for three months against Edward I of England and a powerful army.

The Stuart family made the castle a royal residence and it was a favorite abode of the Jameses, several of whom were born in it. In one corner of the palace is shown the room where James II assassinated the Earl of Douglas, whose body was thrown out of the window and interred in what is now called Douglas' garden. In 1797, the skeleton was found in digging. In the battlement wall of the castle is a small hole through which Queen Mary used to look out, and over it are her initials.

On the spot where Queen Victoria once stood and viewed the scenery are carved her initials and the date, and also those of the Prince and Princess of Wales, who were there later. On the south side of the castle is a cemetery with fine statues of Knox, Henderson and other reformers, and of Ebenezer Erskine, the founder of the United Presbyterian Church, and an exquisite group of statuary representing Margaret, the young female martyr who was tied to a stake and left to be overflowed by the tide, teaching the Scriptures to a younger sister, with an angel bending over them.   On one side of the cemetery stands Greyfriar's Church, a very fine specimen of old architecture, which has many historical associations of which I cannot speak.   About a mile distant from Stirling is the old ruin of Cambuskenneth Abbey, the tower of which still stands.   A pleasant walk, and a ferry across the Forth bring one to it.   Near the high altar were found in digging the bones of James III, who was killed in battle, as already said.   Last year Queen Victoria caused them to be enclosed in a stone monument erected at her expense, " in honor," as the inscription says, " of the remains of my ancestor."

At Dunfermline, further down the Forth, I also held a successful meeting.   Here, too, are the remains of an abbey and palace and tower founded by Malcolm Canmore in the eleventh century.   The ancient town was at an early period the seat of government of Scotland, and a favorite residence of the kings.

> The king sits in Dunfermline town
> Drinking the blood-red wine.

The palace was one of great magnificence and was the birthplace of Charles I. Charles II lived in it for some time and there he subscribed the League and Covenant in 1650. The Abbey is one of the oldest in Scotland, and within its walls were buried numerous kings and queens, and among the rest Robert the Bruce in 1329. When the workmen were digging for the foundations of the modern church building, Bruce's coffin was found and the skeleton entire with parts of the silk shroud. The remains were re-interred under the present pulpit, and on the top of the square tower in immense stone letters one reads, " King Robert the Bruce," each word occupying one of the four sides. A considerable part of the old Abbey Church is preserved entire. It is with indescribable emotions that one walks around such edifices and reflects on the days of old and the personages and scenes that have been connected with them.

While at Stirling, I improved a day of leisure to make a hasty excursion to Loch Lomond, the queen of the Scottish lakes. Taking the railway train about seven in the morning, in about two hours I was at Balloch at the foot of the Loch. Here a small steamer was in waiting on which I embarked and in about two hours and a half was at the head of the Loch. Nothing can surpass the scenery of this beautiful lake which is about twenty-five miles long and at the lower end five miles wide, but narrowing down at the upper end to a mere strip of water. It is full of islands, and from its shores rise high hills and mountains, the chief of which is Ben Lomond, whose head is often lost in the clouds. As the boat plows its way up you often think you are at the end of the route since there seems to be no opening before you, but winding around behind some islands, she finds a passage and moves on. On one side is seen Rob Roy's cave, where tradition says many a captive has been confined. Near the head of the Loch is Inversnaid, where is a cataract, the scene of Wordsworth's poem, " The Highland Girl."

Robert the Bruce is the monarch who, of all that have reigned in Scotland, is most venerated. Wallace is regarded as the William Tell of this land. My earliest recollections are associated with their names in story and history. The Scottish Chiefs was a favorite book of my youth. Hence I feel a special interest in these scenes.

CHAPTER XXIX

LONDON.

Passing through Edinburgh on my way here, I called on Lady Emma Campbell, sister of the Duke of Argyle, and found her a very pleasant and affable lady. On leaving she handed me a contribution for the freedmen. While in Glasgow I attended a meeting of the Bible Society at which the Duke of Argyle presided, and he made an able address. On my way to London, via Liverpool, I preached for the freedmen at the latter place, and am to spend several weeks in England, preaching on Sundays for the freedmen, and speaking on week evenings at public meetings. My engagement with the Missionary Association will close in February, and I have written them that I wish to make an excursion on the continent, and they must send some one to take up the work in my place.

From here I have remitted to New York

$1,500 which, with $3,000 sent a few days ago from Edinburgh, will make, with what previously has been remitted, about $6,750; and there will be probably half as much more. This, I think, is doing pretty well for the short time spent in Scotland. Secretary Strieby writes me that the Committee of the Association are highly gratified with my success, and perfectly satisfied with my work. This, of course, is very pleasant. The people here think I perform wonders.

Yesterday (Sunday) was the day appointed for simultaneous collections for the freedmen in the Congregational churches of England and Wales. I preached for the first time in this great city, in the forenoon, in Dr. Raleigh's chapel. He was one of the English delegates to our Boston Council in 1865, of which I was also a member. His chapel was crowded, including the aisles, and we got $560. In the evening I preached in the old Weigh House Chapel of Rev. T. Binney, who is one of the oldest and most influential and well-known ministers of the Congregational Union. The collection amounted to $250, making the amount at the two places worth in New York $1,100. At the close of the service, Mr. Binney complimented me, and said, "He made out a capital case, and moved me exceedingly, and pulled out of my pocket more money than I had intended to give." In the plate was a note from three little children, with a shilling and three farthings, "for the poor negroes." A little before the opening of the service, I was sitting with Mr. Binney and a few other gentlemen in his study, and I said to him, "Perhaps you would like to have me precede my address with some more strictly religious remarks." With a twinkle in his eye he looked up and replied, "I have done some little preaching there, and I think you had better enter at once on your subject." Of course I did so.

On Saturday next I go to Birmingham to preach for a church that postponed its collection, and the Sunday following to Manchester, for a similar case. On Friday of this week I am to address a public meeting at Tottingham, and am advertised to speak on Tuesday next at Bath, to the congregation formerly ministered to by the well known Rev. William Jay. A letter has just come from the editor of the *Boston Recorder*, for which I am writing a series of letters, and he says he is much pleased with them and is publishing them all.

He adds, " Rev. A. P. Marvin is sitting by, and says, ' the letters are excellent, and much better than those we usually get.' "

MONDAY, 8 p. m.

I have just returned from the monthly tea-meeting of the Congregational ministers of London and vicinity. There were about fifty present. Mr. Binney presided, and introduced me, and alluded in a flattering manner to my address in his chapel the evening previous. I was invited to address the meeting on American affairs, and I did so, of course explaining the case of the freedmen. I spoke for an hour or more, when a vote of thanks to me was passed, and of sympathy in the work for the freedmen. This will open the way for more invitations to preach. Mr. Binney handed me $50, which he said had been contributed in addition to the $250 given in his chapel.

BIRMINGHAM.

I remained a few days in London, partly occupied with freedmen's matters, partly with writing, and partly with sightseeing. I remitted to New York what is equal there to $700, and also $750 received from a lady to whom I wrote in Glasgow. My few weeks in Scotland have yielded $10,000, and perhaps more. While in London I heard a lecture by the Lord Chamberlain (a Congregationalist) at a large meeting of the Friends, given at their request, in which he vindicated the Plymouth Pilgrims from the charge of having persecuted, and a resolution was adopted accepting his views. In the Crystal Palace I saw the bark of one of the California "big trees" set up as large as life.

On my way from London to Birmingham, where I was to preach, I spent a day at Stratford-on-Avon, Shakespeare's town. I shall not undertake to give details of my visit there, since so much has been written of the place; sufficient to say, I saw all the curiosities and *memorabilia*, and passed over the foot-path that Shakespeare trod to Ann Hathaway's cottage. She was the village belle and afterwards Shakespeare's wife. Everything in the cottage remains as it was in their day.

I preached here (Birmingham) on Sunday morning in what was J. A. James' Chapel, now Dr. Dale's, and received $500. In the evening I addressed an immense audience in what resembled a theatre with two galleries, one above the other, crowded full. I did not learn what was the pecuniary response. On

Monday, as I had two days at command, I resolved to run up to Litchfield to see the fine cathedral of which I had heard much. My trip to Litchfield cost me only one and three pence, third class. The cathedral has two of the finest spires in the kingdom and some very beautiful statues; one by Chantry on the tomb of two children, perfectly exquisite and lifelike. I saw the house old Dr. Johnson was born in, and there is a fine statue of him. There Dr. Darwin wrote "Zoomania." There is the free school in which Johnson, Garrick, Addison, and other eminent men received the rudiments of their education. Gloucester being on my way to Bath, I stopped there to spend the night, and the next day to see another very grand cathedral, not so beautiful as that at Litchfield, but more imposing and massive. It has the highest square tower in England, 225 feet, and from the top is a magnificent view. It has the largest window in England, and is old (1445) and fine. The window is eighty-seven feet high and thirty-five wide, and contains one ton and fifteen hundred weight of glass. The deanery is the oldest standing house in the kingdom. Here George Whitefield and Robert Raikes were born. The house still stands in which

Bishop Hooper slept the night before he was burned. In a couple of hours I reached here and was entertained by an ardent friend of the freedmen, who had arranged for the meeting I was to address.

Bath is a great watering-place and one of the most beautiful of cities. Here the celebrated William Jay was a minister. I expect to have a meeting in Bristol, and shall visit Salisbury and Winchester on my way back to London, and see two more of the finest of the numerous cathedrals. I am to speak at Manchester again next Sabbath, and attend a meeting somewhere every evening of the following week. So you see I *work* as well as see sights.

CHAPTER XXX

MANCHESTER, Jan. 27, 1866.

I wrote you last from Bath. Well, on Tuesday evening I addressed a public meeting there for an hour or more with much freedom and, I was told, with good effect. I was interrupted by a southern sympathizer and pro-slavery man, who disputed sóme of my statements; but I was not discomposed, and was ready for him. I triumphantly maintained my position, and was sustained by a hearty vote of thanks by the meeting, and was enabled thus to say some things.that I wished to state. The next morning before light I took the train for Salisbury, and spent the forenoon at the cathedral, one of the most perfect in England, and walked about the town. I then ran down by rail almost to Southampton, and reached Winchester, where is another grand cathedral, a hospital one thousand four hundred years old, and a school of about the same date. Winchester was one of the first settled towns in England, and there Alfred the Great and Canute are buried. It was for a long time the capital of England. The architecture of the cathedral is old Norman. So you see that from Monday morning of this week, I went from Birmingham via Litchfield, Gloucester, Bath, Salisbury, and Winchester to London, and saw four of the finest of the English cathedrals!

On my way here from London, I passed through Buckinghamshire, which county has been the residence of many eminent men, as Milton, Hampden, Herschell, John Newton, Cowper, etc. I stopped at Olney for a time, the residence of one of England's sweetest poets, Cowper. I found the house in which the poet lived with Mrs. Unwin, and was kindly permitted to visit the rooms which he occupied, and was pointed especially to the one where he kept, and amused himself with, his pet hares. Behind the house, in Cowper's day, were the garden and the summer-house where he used to sit, and often met his friend, Rev. John Newton. Like all such places that I have visited, the walls, seats, etc., are covered, every inch, with names and among the rest are those of Lord Macaulay, Baptist Noel, and George B. Cheever. Adjoining the garden is an orchard which separates it from the vicarage in which Newton lived. This is called the "Guinea Orchard" because Cowper paid a guinea a year for the privilege of crossing it at his pleasure for intercourse with Newton.

Passing the vicarage, one comes, in a few hundred yards, to the church where Newton officiated. It is a fine, spacious, stone edifice, with a tall and graceful spire, and has a chime of bells of remarkably fine tone and harmony. In the churchyard are many very old and moss-covered stones. The church was founded in the thirteenth century. Not far off is a bridge with many arches, alluded to in the "Task,"

> That with its wearisome, but needful length,
> Bestrides the wintry flood.

The vicinity of the village furnished the poet many of his delightful descriptions of rural scenery. There is nothing grand like that of the lake district, as the country is flat, but there is a quiet beauty that is pleasant, and in summer the trees and hedges and highly cultivated fields, must be very attractive. Yardley Oak, of which Cowper wrote, still stands at some distance from the town.

In Olney, Cowper "spent nearly twenty years of mingled sorrow and joy. There first his poetical powers were fully developed; there he passed through unfathomed abysses of darkness and despair; and there, under the discipline of God's hand, and the guidance of God's grace, the most precious and perfect fruit of his genius bloomed, and was ripened."

It was an unspeakable blessing to the poet that he was there associated with one of the most excellent ministers then living, who was in every way fitted, notwithstanding the slurs of Southey, to guide and comfort him. The readers of Cowper's memoirs are familiar with the remarkable providence that brought them together. Newton began, but never finished, a sketch of Cowper's life, after the death of the latter, and in it he says: "For nearly twelve years we were seldom separated for seven hours at a time, when we were awake and at home. The first six I passed daily in admiring and attempting to imitate him; during the second six I walked pensively with him in the valley of the shadow of death. He loved the poor. He often visited them in their cottages, conversed with them in the most condescending manner, sympathized with them, counseled and comforted them in their distresses; and those who were seriously disposed were often cheered and animated by his prayers." With what interest I walked over the ground so often traversed by Cowper in his visits to his friend, looked on the house in which they spent so much time together, and tried to imagine how he appeared as he set off on his visits to the poor, I need not say.

Here, too, it was that the "Olney Hymns" were composed, some of the finest in our language, and so descriptive, many of them, of Cowper's varying states of mind, that one must be perfectly familiar with his history and moods, fully to appreciate their power. Southey laments that his genius was not exercised in something else besides devotional poetry, while under Newton's influence! But Dr. Cheever well remarks: "If he had never written a single line beyond the four or five hymns in the Olney Collection, beginning, 'The Spirit breathes upon the Word,' 'Far from the World, O Lord, I Flee,' 'O, for a closer Walk with God,' 'God Moves in a Mysterious Way,' and 'There is a Fountain Filled with Blood,' the gift of those hymns to the Church of God by Cowper's sanctified genius, through Newton's instrumentality, would have been a greater and more precious gift for literature and religion, than, perhaps, all Southey's voluminous writings put together." It is to be feared that Southey knew nothing of the joy and grief of Cowper's religious experience.

Who can ever tire of the exquisite passage in the Task, under the title, "The Garden," beginning,

> I was a stricken deer, that left the herd
> Long since ; with many an arrow deep infixed
> My panting side was charged, when I withdrew
> To seek a tranquil death in distant shades.
> There was I found by One who had himself
> Been hurt by the archers.   In his side he bore,
> And in his hands and feet, the cruel scars.
> With gentle force soliciting the darts,
> He drew them forth, and heal'd and bade me live.

How noble, too, the energetic lines in his poem on " Charity," in which he gives his first utterance of his abhorrence of slavery.

> Oh, most degrading of all ills that wait
> On man, a mourner in his best estate !
> All other sorrows virtue may endure,
> And find submission half a cure.
>
> *   *   *   *   *
>
> A Briton knows, or, if he knows it not,
> The Scripture placed within his reach, he ought

> That *souls* have no *discriminating hue*,
> Alike important in their Maker's view;
>
>   *   *   *   *   *
>
> The wretch that works and weeps without relief
> Has ONE that notices his silent grief,
> He from whose hands alone all power proceeds,
> *Ranks its abuse among the foulest deeds*,
> Considers *all* injustice with a frown,
> But *marks* that man who treads his fellow down.

And how strikingly has this assertion and the following, been verified in our own land of late !

> Remember, *Heaven has a revenging rod*;
> To smite the poor is treason against God.

But I must not quote more. It was with special and peculiar interest that I visited Olney, not only because of my admiration of Cowper and Newton, but also because they are associated with my earliest recollections of home.

My mother read few books, and among them were Cowper's Letters and John Newton's Works, and these were always at hand, and perused and reperused, and often talked about. The latter was her oracle in religion, next to the Bible, and hundreds of times have I heard her remark, " Mr. Newton says so and so." With what deep emotion, were she

now living, would she read what I could say
about the spot in England of highest interest
to her, where Cowper and Newton lived!

After Newton vacated the parsonage, it
was occupied by Lady Austen for a couple
of years. The door was still kept open by
which Cowper communicated with its tenants,
and he was very intimate with this family.
Lady Austen was fruitful in expedients to
animate and please Cowper's mind. It was
she that suggested to him the ballad of John
Gilpin, by repeating to him the tale, with a
merriment and humor that enchanted him to
such an extent that he declared he was kept
awake nearly all night by laughter produced
by the recollection of the story. The next
day he put it into poetry. It was published
anonymously, and was recited to crowded
audiences nightly in London. The profits
of the recitations amounted to £800. Newton
wrote him that his "famous horseman was
giving infinite amusement in London." But
alas, he could only say in reply, "The grin-
ners at 'John Gilpin' little dream what the
author sometimes suffers."

My lodgings in London are in the street
next to Southampton Row, where his uncle
lived while Cowper was apprenticed in that

city in early life, with a view to his becoming
a lawyer! A strange lawyer he would have
made, truly! This uncle had a beautiful
daughter, and her charms seem, from his
biography, to have made a deep impression
upon him. At that time he wrote the lines
descriptive of himself, beginning,

> William was once a bashful youth;
>   His modesty was such,
> That one might say (to say the truth)
>   He rather had too much.

His last letter was written to his dearest
friend, Mr. Newton, and in 1800, on the 25th
of April, he died peacefully, his countenance
settling into calmness and composure, mingled as it were with holy surprise, and this
we are told " was regarded as an index of the
last thoughts and enjoyments of his soul in its
gradual escape from the depths of that inscru-
table despair in which it had been so long
shrouded."

About one o'clock I bade adieu to the interesting little village whose name is so widely
known from its associations with Cowper and
Newton, but which otherwise would be one of
the obscurest in England, and set off for
Northampton.

The ride of twelve miles from Olney to

Northampton is by an excellent road, through a fine, level, and highly cultivated section, passing several villages. I found the last-named town to be of far more importance than I had supposed. I was attracted thither by the interest I felt in it as the place where the celebrated Dr. Doddridge was settled as pastor of a Congregational Church, and where he wrote his excellent " Expositor " of the New Testament, " Rise and Progress," etc., and maintained his Academy, or Training School for Ministers. In a previous letter, I have alluded to the association of Cowper and Newton with my earliest recollections of home, they being special favorites of my mother. I remember, too, that Doddridge's " Expositor " was the *one* book of my father, so far as the interpretation of the New Testament was concerned. I can see it now in several old volumes bearing marks of constant use, as it stood in the bookcase with glass doors, or lay upon the table of the family sitting-room when I was a boy. It was used in family worship, and its " Improvements " were read in connection with the text. How often have I heard my venerated father quote " Dr. Doddridge," and as often my mother, " Mr. Newton " !

I was fortunate on my arrival at Northampton to meet Rev. Mr. Arnold, one of the successors of Doddridge in the pastorate of the old Independent Church; there are several other churches there now. He at once took me to the chapel where Doddridge formerly preached. It is a plain, stone building, without belfry or spire. It has been lengthened to double its original extent, but the style of architecture has been preserved. The original vestry has been kept intact, where prayer-meetings were held and where the good man used to spend hours alone in meditation and prayer. There are also the plain armchair and table which he used; and hung up in a frame on the wall is the original manuscript "call" of the church extended to Dr. Doddridge to become its pastor, with his answer. The pew which Colonel Gardiner occupied is also pointed out.

On what is now one of the principal streets of the town, stands the long, two-story building, with stone front, where Doddridge lived and gave instruction to his students. If is used at present for business purposes. In his day the place did not contain more than five or six thousand inhabitants, and his chapel, which was then in a central position, is now considered on one side of the town.

As I have already intimated, I was chiefly attracted to Northampton because of its associations with Doddridge, to whose " Rise and Progress," instrumentally, I owe, in a great degree, my conversion, but I found, on conversing with Rev. Mr. Arnold, that there is much of historic interest connected with the place and its vicinity. About fourteen miles distant is the famous field of Naseby, where one of Cromwell's great and decisive battles was fought, and the house still stands, and was shown me, in which he slept the night before the engagement. Near here, also, was fought an important battle between Henry II and his barons, and I walked over the site and saw a few remaining ruins of an important castle—the one in which Henry and Thomas à Becket had a long conference, as recorded in history.

In the town I was shown an old church, which affords the finest specimen I have yet seen of rich and ornamental Norman architecture. The tower is very fine, and the interior arches are finished with much care and skill, with zigzag ornamentation. Ruskin once visited the place and expressed great admiration of the building. It is superior in some of its parts to anything I have seen even in the cathedrals of the period.

Northampton was the residence of the well-known Baptist minister, Dr. Ryland, and near by is the village of Kettering, where Andrew Fuller was settled, and where Carey, the pioneer missionary, lived and worked at his trade of shoemaking. A mile or two distant, also, is the church of which Hervey was rector, and the village where he wrote his "Meditations," and "Theron and Aspasio."

Leaving Northampton about five in the afternoon, I next day proceeded on to Manchester, where I spent the Sabbath, occupying two Congregational pulpits in pleading the cause of the freedmen. One of the congregations responded with a contribution of £100, or $500. The amount collected at the other I did not learn.

CHAPTER XXXI

COVENTRY—REV. SAMUEL MARTIN—OPENING
OF PARLIAMENT — THE QUEEN — BUNHILL
FIELDS CEMETERY— GREENWICH —EXTEN-
SION OF MY TIME IN GREAT BRITAIN—
NOTTINGHAM

LONDON, February 2d.

I reached here again to-day. From Manchester I went to Birmingham and arranged with the secretary of the Aid Society, to hold several meetings in that vicinity with him. At Coventry I spoke in a large hall, being entertained by a hospitable family of Friends, and fared well, as usual. In the morning half a dozen ministers were invited to meet me at a sumptuous breakfast. There are here two fine old churches, one built in 1440. One of them has a spire 303 feet high, pronounced by Sir Christopher Wren, the architect of St. Paul's, the most beautiful he ever saw. We next visited Rugby, the place of Tom Brown's school days, as written by Hughes, and had a good meeting, Dr. Temple, now archbishop of Canterbury, in the chair.

I have just got a letter from Secretary Strieby

of New York that upsets all my plans for the Continent. He urges me to spend the summer here, and thinks that by so doing I can make up my collections to $50,000. He urges strong reasons, and says that no one else can do as much now as I can. The same thing is urged here by the friends of our cause. Mr. Strieby offers to go and supply my pulpit, if necessary, and says he shall go to Homer and get the consent of the church to extend my time.

LONDON, February 7.

The Missionary Association at New York has agreed to pay for the supply of my pulpit if I will remain here longer. I long to be at home among my people and at my legitimate work. On Sunday last I did not preach, though urged to do so; I preferred to rest. I heard Rev. Samuel Martin, one of the most spiritual of our ministers, preach in the finest dissenting chapel I have seen, beautiful and spacious, with two galleries, and accommodating three thousand people, in the most genteel part of the city. On Monday, having leisure, I visited the British Museum.

I happened to be in London on what is considered one of the great days, the day when parliament is opened by the sovereign in person. Of course I went, with everybody else, to see the procession move from Buckingham palace to the Parliament house. The queen was alone in her royal coach, the Prince and Princess of Wales preceding. She had eight cream-colored horses. I had a good view of her Majesty as she leaned forward and bowed, and also of the Prince and Princess of Wales. We saw the third generation of royalty. I endeavored in vain to get a ticket to the House of Lords. There was, it was said, a grand array of peers and peeresses richly dressed and glittering in diamonds, with ministers from foreign states, among whom the Turkish ambassador was one of the most gay. The queen looked in remarkably good health, but was very sober and seemed to take but little interest in the scenes that were taking place. Her grief at the loss of her husband scarcely seems to be lessened at all by the lapse of time. It is very touching to see her true womanly devotedness to Albert, surnamed "The Good." It is said that after his death she once exclaimed, "There will be no one now to call me Victoria!" It has been truly said that "had she lived in the mediæval ages she would have been honored in her lifetime, and canonized after death for those sublime qualities which are so conspicuously illustrated in her life and character." Amid all the corruptions of a court she is spotless, and as a mother she is a model. Who then can wonder at the devoted loyalty of all her subjects? She has sorrowed like a true woman, and her great grief gives her new grace and dignity.

A day or two after the opening of parliament I obtained from Mr. Adams, our minister, a ticket to the House of Commons and spent an evening there. I had pointed out to me Gladstone, D'Israeli, and other distinguished men.

To-day I visited one of the most interesting spots in London, to an American and a descendant of the Puritans, Bunhill burying-ground. It is entirely filled and contains six thousand and ten graves. With what emotions of interest and reverence did I walk through the sacred precincts and stand beside the graves of its occupants! Among them I read the names of Isaac Watts, Bunyan the glorious dreamer, John Owen, the mother of the Wesleys, De Foe, author of the most popular boy's book ever written, "Robinson Crusoe," Drs. Gill, Ripon, Fleetwood, Dr. Priestly, the martyrs of 1684, and others. The sexton as he showed me about would say in lugubrious tones, " There lies poor Bunyan," and " Poor old De Foe, there he is," and " Owen, poor fellow, that's his grave!" I copied the following from some of the inscriptions:

> The world's a city full of crooked streets ;
> Death 's the market-place where all men meet ;
> If life were merchandise which men could buy,
> The rich would live—but the poor must die.

Another, Dame Mercy Page, wife of a baronet :

In 67 months she was tapped 65 times and had taken away 240 gallons of water, without ever repining or ever fearing the operation.

The old sexton seemed very proud of the place and often spoke of " our having here the great" so-and-so. In one funeral, he said, there were seventy mourning carriages. He said all Americans came there and all wanted to see De Foe's grave. But I felt more interest in those of Watts and Bunyan. Afterwards I made a visit to the scene of Cowper's poetical and humorous tale of " John Gilpin," and saw the inn from which he started on his famous ride.

LONDON, February 9.

I had planned to start for the Continent about the first of March, and after a short trip at once to leave for home. But all may be changed. I have written Dr. Strieby that if I am to remain here longer he must fully satisfy my church, and have it understood that the proposition to lengthen my absence does not come from me. I am not unmindful of their interests, and if I stay it will be from a sense of duty only. You must correct the impression that you say is felt by some, that I shall not settle down again in Homer. I much prefer a pastorate to any agency.

To-day, having leisure, I ran down to Greenwich, the great naval station, and visited the famous observatory, the hospital, and a hall full of naval pictures, portraits, etc.; a very interesting place. On my return I found awaiting me a remittance of $1,000 from Scotland, and am getting sums to send to New York by almost every steamer.

I spoke in Exeter hall last evening, where there was a great gathering. Well, I see it is settled that I am to continue longer in this work. The conduct of my church and the feeling manifested gratify me exceedingly, and I do not mean to strain the bond between my people and myself.

I preached last Sabbath at Nottingham, where there is a Congregational college, and received $125. I have two meetings to attend in this vicinity this week.

CHAPTER XXXII

I visited some places of deep interest to Congregationalists: Old Boston, Scrooby, and Austerfield. Passing through Lincoln I stopped to see a fine old cathedral, and reached Boston, where the celebrated John Cotton, afterwards settled in our Boston, Massachusetts, once preached. From this port the Pilgrims originally attempted to embark for Holland, but were arrested and prevented from doing so. The church edifice has an extremely high tower which was formerly used as a lighthouse. Entering the building I ascended the pulpit stairs and stood for a few moments where Cotton preached. He became, as you know, a staunch Congregationalist in America.

From Boston I went to Scrooby and Austerfield and stood on the consecrated ground where the fathers of Congregationlism in America worshiped, and then took a stroll over the foot-path to Austerfield on which Bradford used to visit Scrooby. At Auster-field still stands the little, quaint, old stone church in which he was baptized, and there I saw the identical font, and the parchment record in which his baptism is inscribed. I also saw the house in which he lived.

At Bawtry, the railway station adjoining Scrooby, I became acquainted with Charles Lawther, Esq., who was occupying the house belonging to Lord Houghton (Monck-ton Milnes, the poet), the lord of the manor in which Scrooby is included. I was invited to spend the night with Mr. Lawther's family, and was very hospitably entertained. I found them much interested in Congregationalism in America. In conjunction with them, I arranged to have a stone from the Scrooby mansion house sent to Chicago, to be inserted in the front wall of the new edifice of the New England Church, a piece of Plymouth rock to be placed on the opposite side of the entrance.

Returning to Birmingham I spoke on two evenings at freedmen's meetings. I have engagements to speak at Peckham Rye and at Camberwell, both parts of London, and also at Bristol and Chelmsford.

LONDON.

I took a run to Hampton Court, the grand old palace of Henry VIII, and saw fine paintings and beautiful grounds. I was invited to act as chaplain at the celebration of Washington's birthday in London, but could not accept, as I had another engagement. Deacon Hawley of Homer writes me that the women of my church voted *unanimously* against extending my leave of absence. This is flattering to me, I am sure. I would much rather be at home, as I am working so hard, but March is the best month for my operations.

I did not preach on Sunday, but went to hear Rev. L. Bevan, a young man, at Tottenham Chapel, Whitefield's old place, and was much pleased. The young man will make his mark.[1] In the evening I went to St. Paul's and heard the archbishop of York. The sermon was not remarkable, but the

---

[1] This has been fulfilled, for this was the future Rev. Dr. Bevan, who once labored with the Brick Church in New York, and afterwards became a famous Congregational leader in Australia.

crowd was immense, some nine thousand under the dome, which was lighted by one thousand gas-jets. The dome is one hundred feet high. The scene was very striking; the frescoes were finely displayed.

Thursday I went to Rotherham, near Sheffield, where is a Congregational theological seminary, or college, as they say here. I spoke at a freedmen's meeting and dined with the faculty and students. I also had, afterwards, a delightful day at Cambridge, the seat of one of the great universities. I walked about the beautiful town, and saw fine paintings and statuary. Here Lord Bacon, Sir Isaac Newton, and others of the great men of England were educated, and it is especially interesting to Americans because John Robinson, the pastor of the Pilgrims, and many Puritan divines were students here. There is here the finest statue of Newton in England.

In going to Cambridge I passed through Huntington, the birthplace of Cromwell, and St. Ives, where he once lived as a farmer. I also passed Bradford, where was the jail in which Bunyan was confined and wrote his immortal Pilgrim's Progress: also Sherwood Forest, famous for Robin Hood's exploits.

There is something of interest everywhere in England.

I have recently been to Bristol, where I spoke at a freedmen's meeting. I was the guest of a family of Friends, and, as usual, was royally entertained. The next day my host, who lives near Mueller's Orphan Houses, took me over to see them. There are about eleven hundred orphans, and Mr. Mueller is about erecting buildings for nine hundred more.

On Saturday I went seventeen miles to Brentwood, and preached twice in the Congregational chapel. Monday evening I am advertised to speak at Stoke Newington in the northern part of London, and on Thursday at Chelmsford. So you see my hands are full. Dr. Strieby writes me that the committee at New York are highly satisfied with my labors and their results. This is, of course, encouraging. But I often think of my own congregation, and wish I could address them. I am much pressed for time often in London, distances are so great and days so short. A single call sometimes takes half a day. I sit up frequently till 11 o'clock at night, and last night I did not fall asleep till 1 o'clock.

You allude to the President's course (Andrew Johnson). It is injuring us somewhat here, and I fear the interest in the freedmen is somewhat declining. My correspondence is very heavy with you, and the papers, and all over the kingdom.

I spoke lately at a meeting where Thomas Hughes presided (author of "Tom Brown"), and he made a speech.

LONDON, March 21.

I went down to Chelmsford and had a very successful meeting, having the whole evening. I spoke an hour and a half in a crowded hall, and received what in New York will be worth $400. I send a paper with a very flattering report, calling mine "a masterly address!"

The next day I went to Colchester and arranged to preach on the Sabbath and have a public meeting on Monday evening. Having leisure, I went to Ipswich, Stowemarket, and Bury St. Edmunds, the last place made notable by Dickens. Returning to Colchester, I preached on Sunday to a large congregation, and in the evening took for my subject, "The Good Samaritan," applying it to the case of the freedmen, and on Monday evening spoke an hour and a half at a public meeting.

I enjoyed this trip very much, as this was the region from which came the first settlers of the Massachusetts colony, Hooker, Eliot, the Indian apostle, Shepard of Cambridge, etc. · The towns thereabout have the same names as those in, Eastern Massachusetts: Chelmsford, Billerica, Braintree, Needham, Dedham, etc. At Colchester are old Roman towers, castles, etc. Constantine, the great emperor of Rome, once lived there. His mother was the daughter of the British princess, Helena, and the walls of a church she founded and endowed are still standing. There are many antiquities here. In that section I found a town of Holbrooke, indicating clearly from whence came my ancestors.

LONDON, March 28.

The Missionary Association at New York have arranged with Rev. Dr. W. W. Patton to come over and release me, and I have, therefore, decided to start at once for the Continent to spend a few weeks, returning in time to go with him to Scotland and introduce him, and with him meet the different Presbyterian Assemblies which hold their annual sessions in Edinburgh. My people at home have become so impatient at my absence that my plans are changed.   I expect now to sail from Liverpool June 2 (D. V.).

As so much has been written and published by tourists on the Continent, I will not quote from my correspondence while there, but will simply give an itinerary of my journey. Most of what I have quoted before related to places not often visited by American tourists, or which were connected with my work.

CHAPTER XXXIII

I left London the second day of April, and
crossed the channel from New Haven to
Dieppe in France. Awaking the next morning after leaving London, having had a quiet
passage, I found myself for the first time in
my life among a people of a foreign tongue.
However, I found the knowledge I had acquired, in early life, of the French language
of advantage to me, and I managed to secure
a good breakfast at a hotel near by. I then
took passage on the railway for Paris, via
Rouen, through Normandy, and found the
trip delightful. The weather was like June
at home, and my first view of *La Belle
France* was exceedingly pleasant.

I spent a few days in Paris visiting the
principal places and objects of interest, as the
palaces and galleries of painting and statuary,
Notre Dame cathedral, the Jardin des Plants,
Bois du Boulogne, Napoleon's tomb, and
taking a run out to Versailles, with its mag-

nificent palace and paintings, the cottage of
Madame de Maintenon, etc.

From Paris I went south by rail, and then
crossed the Alps by the Mont Cenis pass, the
tunnel not then being constructed, to Turin,
the former capital of Savoy. From thence I
proceeded to Milan, with its splendid cathedral of many spires and hundreds of statues,
visited some galleries of paintings and saw
the original of Leonardo da Vinci's " Last
Supper."

Bologna was the next stopping place and
then Florence. And what shall I say of the
few days there, the seat of so much art and
culture and with such a history? It would
require volumes to describe the extensive art
galleries, the famous Duomo, or cathedral,
whose dome suggested that of St. Peter's at
Rome, the Campanile and Baptistry, with its
carved bronze doors, and the wondrous scenery of the place.

Taking the railway again, I reached Pisa,
with its leaning tower, which I ascended, and
its Campo Santo, and church ; then to Leg-
horn, and at last to Rome. I cannot describe
the sensation I felt, when, on reaching the
station, I heard the conductor cry out,
" ROMA ! " Could it be that I was dreaming,

or was I really at last in the ancient capital of the world, of which I had read so much in history and the descriptions of travelers? But I soon woke to the fact that I was really there and to the anticipation of the sights that were to break upon me in that city. I spent some eight days where months and years would be required to exhaust the wonders of the city. Of course I visited St. Peter's and climbed up into its dome; saw the statue of St. Peter, whose brazen toe has been so reduced in size by the kisses of devout Catholics; entered the Vatican and roamed through the rooms filled with paintings and statuary; saw Raphael's great painting of the Last Judgment, and spent no little time in the numerous galleries of art in the city. The Forum, Capitoline Hill, the Colosseum, the arches of Titus and Constantine, and the Catacombs, each and all claimed a visit, and especially I was interested at the church of St. John Lateran, where Luther climbed the stairs on his knees and first realized that we are justified by faith and not by works.

From Rome I next went to Naples, with its unequaled bay of crescent shape, and near by the great volcano of Vesuvius, which I ascended and then descended into its crater, which was then undisturbed. At the foot of the mountain I wandered through the streets of Pompeii, built more than twenty centuries before and then being excavated. In the museum I was also much interested by the vast number of antiquities that were preserved there, rescued from the ruins of Pompeii. It was astonishing to see how many household and other articles there resembled those now in use.

At Naples, which was the extreme point of my journey, I embarked on a steamer, and reached Genoa, the city of marble palaces, where there is a fine large statue of Columbus. Here are manufactured beautiful cameos, some specimens of which I obtained. From Genoa I again reached Milan, and from there proceeded to the beautiful Lago Maggiore, which I crossed to the foot of the Alps, and the entrance to the wonderful St. Gothard pass, which Napoleon constructed for his army to invade Italy. The tunnel for the railway, since constructed, was not then in existence. We began the ascent by diligence until we reached the snow level, and there took sledges over the summit. We passed the famous Hospice of St. Bernard, and descending on the other side of the Alps, we reached the plain and saw the spot where, tradition says, William Tell shot, with his arrow, the apple from the head of his son at the command of the tyrant. Crossing Lake Lucerne, with Mt. Pilatus in the distance, we reached the city of that name, where I spent a short time, including a Sunday, and heard a Capuchin friar preach, clad in his peculiar costume, with the cord around his body. At Lucerne is the remarkable sculpture on the face of a huge rock of an immense lion, which has been much admired, the work of a famous artist.

From Lucerne I reached Basel by rail, where is a celebrated institution for educating missionaries, one of whom I knew in Iowa. A delightful railroad trip from Basel took me again to Paris. And, by the way, I noticed that the cars in Switzerland were constructed on the American pattern, instead of the ones I saw in France and England, which have separate compartments. Is it because Switzerland is republican like our own country, and less aristocratic in its ideas? From Paris I hastened back to London to join Rev. Dr. Patton, and with him to attend the meetings of the Presbyterian Assemblies in Edinburgh. To accomplish this I was obliged to shorten my stay on the continent. I intended to return again and visit Germany, but I was not able to carry out this plan. I shall now resume the extracts from my letters to my wife.

CHAPTER XXXIV

EDINBURGH, May 11.

We left London by the East Coast line of
railway, stopping at York to see what is considered the finest cathedral in England, unless
St. Paul's in London is an exception as being
larger and grander but not so elaborate. But
I was disappointed with it, as I had just seen
that at Milan, and St. Peter's at Rome. We
found it very interesting, however. We
also saw the noble old pile at Durham,
massive and grand, standing on the very edge
of a vast precipice overlooking a deep chasm.

Leaving there we stopped at Alynwick,
near Newcastle-upon-Tyne, and viewed the
castle there, the splendid seat of the Duke of
Northumberland (The Percy). On reaching
Edinburgh we began preparing for a hearing

in behalf of the freedmen before the Synod of the United Presbyterians. The Monday following the Assembly of the Free Church and after that that of the Established Church were to meet. I feel much relieved now, and shall fill up the little time remaining to me after the Synod meets, in sightseeing, leaving Dr. Patton to carry on the work. But I find I must give up my proposed return to the Continent, and the trip up the Rhine and into Germany, and hurry home. I have taken my passage on the Cunard steamer *Scotia* from Liverpool for June second.

Edinburgh, May 18.

"We have met the enemy and they are ours." Last evening Dr. Patton and I both addressed the United Presbyterian Synod, by appointment, and we carried all before us! I send a paper with a meagre report. We fully accomplished our object, and, amid much enthusiasm, the Synod adopted a resolution recommending a general and simultaneous collection for our object in all their churches. This will prepare the way for the Free and Established Church meetings, and it will not be necessary for me to remain longer. So I am about through with my mission. Nothing more can be done here now, until the other bodies meet. So Dr. Patton and I have decided to take a trip up the coast of the Western Highlands by steamer, and passing through the Caledonian canal, reach Inverness, the most northerly city in Scotland.

We have been seeing this city more thoroughly than I had done, and have held one public freedmen's meeting at Dalkeith, about eight miles from here. We both spoke, and the meeting was a success. A committee of ladies was appointed to solicit subscriptions, but I do not know the result. While at Dalkeith we visited the grounds of the Duke of Buccleuch, and his castle. He is the largest landowner in Scotland, and his daily revenue is enormous; I dare not state the amount as reported to us. At any rate, it would enable me easily to bring the year around, and keep out of debt! I imagine he feels no embarrassment for want of funds to meet his necessities with $5,000 a day! He has the finest garden and grounds in the realm. We were shown about the grounds, and through some of the endless conservatories where are grown all tropical fruits.

From Dalkeith we went by rail to Hawthornden, and then walked down the valley of the Esk, which is very wild and romantic, and reached Roslin Chapel, the most exquisite and delicate specimen of mediæval architecture in Great Britain. Returning to Edinburgh, we went in the evening to hear Dickens read one of his inimitable stories, "Dr. Marigold," and also the chapter in the "Pickwick Papers" describing the trial of Mr. Pickwick, which convulsed the audience with laughter. The largest hall was crowded. He must have realized £500. On Sunday Dr. Patton preached for the freedmen in the forenoon, and in the evening we both spoke to a very large audience in the Free Church Assembly room, on the religious aspects of the freedmen's work, and much interest was manifested. This is probably my last public appearance, though I am invited to preach in Liverpool before I sail, but I shall probably not be able to do so.

INVERNESS, May 23.

On Monday morning Dr. Patton and I started on our excursion to the north of Scotland, as there would be a week's interval before the meeting of another Assembly. But before we really started for the north, we made a little detour, and visited the Trossachs and the scenes of the "Lady of the Lake," Scott's most popular poem, and we found his descriptions of the region were very exact and perfect.   He was in the habit of going over the ground where his poems were located.   We saw the place where the famous duel of Fitz James and Rob Roy took place, and Ellen's Isle; crossed Lake Katrine on a small steamer, then took a coach for five miles to Loch Lomond, through which we sailed to the foot of the lake, from whence by rail we reached Glasgow.   It was a day long to be remembered.

At Glasgow we took the steamer on the Clyde to Greenock, where we embarked on an ocean steamer to proceed up the west coast of the Highlands, calling at Oban, from whence visitors depart for the island of Staffa. We regretted that we could not go there, as it was not the proper season for it.   At Corpach, beyond Oban, we left the steamer, and rode a mile to Bannerie, the head of the great Caledonian canal.   There we took a canal boat for this city.   The scenery on our route from Greenock was of exceeding beauty and variety; the mountains, islands, and coast constitute the Highlands of Scotland, so familiar to readers of Scottish history and fiction.   The canal is sixty-four miles in length, or rather the canal proper is twenty miles and the rest of the route is through natural lochs from one to three miles wide and of great beauty. We went ashore at Foyers Falls, the highest in Scotland, being about ninety feet; passed the ancient palace of the Kings of the Scots; saw Ben Nevis, the highest peak in Great Britain; had delightful weather, and on the whole enjoyed the trip exceedingly.

Inverness is a large town, the capital of the Highlands. A little to the north is Cromarty, where Hugh Miller was born and spent his early years. We were so far north that the length of daylight enabled us to read a newspaper easily out-of-doors at 10 o'clock at night. We anticipate great pleasure in returning south by rail on the east side of the Highlands.

CHAPTER XXXV

IRELAND — GIANT'S CAUSEWAY — DUBLIN — MENAI STRAIT — CARNARVON CASTLE — ACROSS NORTH WALES—CHESTER—LIVERPOOL—RETURN TO HOMER

I wrote you last from Inverness, and since then I have made quite a tour in Ireland and Wales. Dr. Patton and I left Inverness by rail for Glasgow, via Perth and Stirling, through fine scenery, crossing the Grampian hills, where Norval's father " fed his flocks," as we used to shout in school days, in our elocutionary exercises. So I have done Scotland pretty well.

At Greenock, the port of Glasgow, we took the steamer for Belfast, Ireland, and from there by rail we visited the celebrated Giant's Causeway, a very great curiosity. The tradition has it, that it is a part of an enormous bridge the giants of old time constructed to unite Ireland and Scotland. You will be interested to read about the locality in the encyclopedia. After exploring the causeway we returned to Belfast, where Dr. Patton left me, to return again to Edinburgh and finish up with the Presbyterian Assemblies.

From Belfast I went to Dublin, where I spent a few days, including a Sunday. It is a splendid city and has many fine edifices. From there I crossed the channel, in five hours, to Holyhead, and thence by the grand tubular bridge, one of our modern " wonders," crossed the Menai Strait to Bangor, in North Wales, at the foot of Mount Snowdon. There are the ruins of several old and celebrated castles in the vicinity, and among them that of Carnarvon, where Edward II of England was born. The Welsh people were very tenacious of the right to be ruled by a *native* prince, and to satisfy them, Edward I sent his queen to this castle, near the birth of her son. There he first saw the light and so was born a Welshman, and when he came to the throne, the Welsh people's demand was satisfied. He was the first heir apparent to the British throne that was created Prince of Wales, the title since of all the eldest sons of reigning British sovereigns.

Carnarvon is one of the noblest ruins in the kingdom, and its walls are still entire and from seven to nine feet thick ; there are thirteen embattled towers, with five, six, or eight sides. The gateway under the great square tower had four portcullises. The town itself was once surrounded with walls and round towers. I spent considerable time exploring these ruins, and in imagination recalling scenes enacted there in the past. Carnarvon is a great watering place on account of its vicinity to the grandest scenery in North Wales. My journey across North Wales was most delightful, the scenery being unsurpassed by any I had seen.

Reaching Chester, near which is Mr. Gladstone's residence, I lingered a considerable time, examining its quaint and peculiar streets, the dwellings and shops of which project over the sidewalks, visiting the cathedral, and walking around on the walls of the town, from which there are fine views of the surrounding country. At length arriving here (Liverpool), my wanderings and labors in Europe are ended, and I am looking forward to a speedy reunion with my family and my congregation. I shall be delighted to settle down again to my loved employment in the pastorate.

Here ends my correspondence.

Leaving Liverpool June 2, after a pleasant passage of nine days, I landed at New York, made my report to the Missionary Association, and hastened to my home in Homer. I was most cordially welcomed by my people, and, I need not add, by my family. Dr. Patton sent a message to my congregation saying, " You must treat him with the greatest respect and consideration for awhile, so as to let him down gradually from the high and commanding position he has held here!" So ended my mission of eight months, an important and, I hope, useful period of my life. It was an unspeakable relief to throw off the responsibility involved, and to return to the more quiet labors of my parish.

CHAPTER XXXVI

My parish at Homer was very extensive,
embracing not only the large village, but
several miles of the vicinity, north, east, and
west. Some of my congregation came from
three to five miles, and one regular attendant
and his family seven miles. I soon became
again absorbed in my pastoral work, and in
addition, as my church was one of the largest in the interior of the state, and centrally
situated, I was called to coöperate with the
agent of the American Home Missionary
Society and others, in the general work of
the denomination in the state, as I was very
ready to do.

Rev. L. Smith Hobart, whom I had known
in the West, had then the supervision of the
society's operations in the interior of New
York, and resided at Syracuse, about forty

miles by rail from Homer. We together edited and published a local monthly religious paper, *The Excelsior*, as a denominational organ, and I aided him in organizing some associations of churches and ministers, and in bringing back some Congregational churches that had either stood alone or had been connected with presbytery. I was called upon for consultation and advice by quite a number of persons in the adjoining large village of Cortland, the county seat, who had become dissatisfied with the government of the Methodists, and wished to form a Congregational church, and this was soon after accomplished. It has become a large and influential one with a fine house of worship. During this period I also secured the well known temperance lecturer, Dr. Charles Jewett, to canvass the county and hold meetings in every town, and he did very effective service.

While I was pastor at Homer, I was invited, with my church, to participate in an ecclesiastical council in Washington city, D. C., to adjust a difficulty which had arisen between the pastor of the First Congregational church there, and his people. I attended with one of my deacons, Mr. E. G. Ranney, as a delegate. Rev. Dr. R. S. Storrs of Brooklyn presided as moderator, and the object was accomplished and harmony restored. While in attendance on that council I was the guest of the Hon. S. P. Chase, Secretary of the Treasury, and thus had an opportunity to make his acquaintance, and was very agreeably entertained. While there, I had an example of General O. O. Howard's conscientiousness and adherence to principles. One day he and the German ambassador dined with the secretary. When the wine decanter was passed around and came to the General, who sat beside me, he declined to fill his glass, as he was a total abstainer, an act, which, in the circumstances, impressed me deeply; but it was characteristic of this noble Christian soldier, who has been called "our American Havelock."

There were several special revival seasons during my pastorate at Homer, and one of peculiar power. I had felt for some time that my church was in need of such a visitation of the Spirit, and had prepared a sermon founded on the charge of the Spirit to the church in Sardis, as recorded in the book of Revelation, 3:1, etc. On Saturday the evangelist, Rev. J. T. Avery, who had held a very successful series of meetings with my church in Dubuque, called at my house, and I invited him to remain over the Sabbath. He did so, and sat with me in the pulpit, while I preached. The sermon proved to be very effective, and at the close of the service I introduced my friend, and stated the fact that he had labored very effectively with my former church, and I proposed that he should be invited to hold a series of meetings with us. A vote was taken, and he was engaged to remain as I suggested. He began his labors the next day, and continued three or four weeks. The result was a most powerful work of grace, and an addition to the church of nearly or quite one hundred persons, and, what was remarkable, among the converts was a very unusual number of people quite advanced in life.

While in Homer I was invited by Rev. Dr. A. F. Beard, pastor then of Plymouth Church in Syracuse, and now Secretary of the American Missionary Association of New York, to assist him in a series of revival meetings in his church. I spent two or three weeks there, preaching each day. God blessed our labors, and there was a large addition to the church. It was a pleasant season, in which the pastor and I worked in perfect harmony.

During my residence in Homer, also, I was invited to deliver an address on revivals at a meeting of the Evangelical Association in Boston, and it was afterwards published in a monthly periodical. I also preached the annual sermon for the Education Society in Boston, which was also published.

In the summer of 1869 I again, with my wife, made a visit to relatives in California, of whom we had quite a circle, in San Francisco, Oakland, and the vicinity. While there I supplied one Sabbath the pulpit of the Congregational Church in Stockton, which was at the time pastorless, and received an invitation to become its pastor. I agreed to take the matter into consideration and to consult my church. There were strong attractions in that direction, as it would bring us near our numerous relatives and friends, the climate was genial, and, moreover, it would seem to open up to me an enlarged and needy field of labor.

On my return home I laid the matter before my church, but they were unwilling to release me. However, they consented to call a council for advice. The council hesitated, the delegate from Syracuse making strong opposition to my dismissal, but finally they decided, for the reasons which I presented, to advise that my resignation should be accepted. This was done, and I notified the church at Stockton that I would accept their call to the pastorate.

Removing then to that city, I was in due time installed by council, and soon became identified with the Congregationalists of California in their work of evangelization in that great state. I was especially interested in the movement to establish the Pacific Theological Seminary in Oakland, and was happy to aid a little in securing the grand site which it now occupies, and, in after years, to coöperate in founding a scholarship, which bears my name, and also to contribute something to its endowment fund. While residing in Stockton I made a very pleasant trip to the southern part of the state and was delighted with the orange groves in that section, which I had never before seen. Taking a steamer at San Francisco, I proceeded down the coast and landed at San Pedro, the port of Los Angeles, and after a few days in that city and vicinity returned to San Francisco by the stage route through the interior, traveling night and day, the railroad between the two cities not having then been constructed.

CHAPTER XXXVII

My very pleasant relations with the Stockton church continued two years, when another of the marked interpositions of Providence in my affairs again unsettled me, and called me back to undertake a very important work in the Empire state. This was to act as secretary of the newly-organized New York State Home Missionary Society, and to inaugurate its work. Rev. W. A. Robinson, for several years president of the society, thus stated the facts as to the organization of that society, in an address which he made at a late meeting of the society. He said:

Rev. L. Smith Hobart, who, from Syracuse, exercised the supervision of Congregational interests in the interior of the state, had been recalled to New York from motives of economy to assist in the office there, but it did not result in enlarged efficiency, and the leaders in the central, northern, and western portions of our commonwealth felt that a different mode of administration was an imperative necessity. After no little conference and discussion, it was deemed best to form a State Home Missionary Society, auxiliary to the National Society. There were peculiar difficulties in the way of doing this, partly because of the notions of economy already alluded to, and partly because the headquarters of the parent society were within the state. But at the meeting of our State Association at Rochester in 1872, such an organization was effected. Rev. Dr. L. Ives Budington, of Brooklyn, was chosen president, Rev. John C. Holbrook secretary, and Rev. E. Taylor, D. D., of Binghamton, vice-president. The secretary was called to our work from California, and after nine years of effective work here returned to that state, where, last winter, he preached a birthday sermon at the advanced age of eighty-six, of great vigor and timeliness. Only two of the first board of trustees are still connected with the society.

Not long before this, as I have stated, I had left the East in the hope of spending my latter years among relatives, in the genial climate and the enjoyment of the luscious fruits of the Golden State. But God still had an important work for me to do elsewhere than in the simple pastorate in which I was then employed. It was urged upon me that a vastly wider field of usefulness would open before me on my return to the East, for which my past experience had fitted me, especially as I was known in the state of New

York, and had become acquainted with its wants. The path of duty then seemed plain, and I resigned my Stockton pastorate, was dismissed by council, and with my family removed to the central city of Syracuse, and entered upon my new work in 1872.

And now began a period of the most severe labors of my life, which continued nine years, until I felt that my advanced age required that I should discontinue it. I resigned, notwithstanding the protest of my associates that I ought to continue. My official duties required of me a great amount of travel through the state, the supervision of the home missionary work, the supplying of ministers for the aided churches that were in need of them, the collection of funds, the reviving of churches that had declined, and as far as possible the reclaiming to our ranks of those which had been brought under the control of presbytery, and the organization of new churches where they were needed. This, it will be seen, would tax all my abilities to the uttermost.

The Plan of Union with the Presbyterians, heretofore alluded to, had operated in this state, as at the West, disastrously to Congregationalism, and prevented Western New

York from becoming almost as Congregational as New England, since it was largely settled from the latter section, and it devolved on me as secretary to rectify the mistakes as far as possible. Rev. Dr. Robinson, in his paper from which I have already quoted, says:

The growth of our denomination in this state, since the organization of this society, not only in the number and strength of our churches, but in the quality of our denominational life, has been very manifest. Twenty-four years ago there was no Congregational church in Buffalo, where now we have five. There was none in Olean, Lysander, Ogdensburg, Oswego Falls (Utica), Cortland, Corning (Schenectady), or Newburg. In the following places where there was but one, now there are two, viz., Albany, Rochester, Middletown, Binghamton, Lockport, and Elmira. In Syracuse we had but one, now five. There has been increased size and vigor in many of our churches, and the associational life has become more fully organized and developed. Our society in its fostering care of the weaker churches and its entering upon new fields, has done not a little to bring about this better state of things. The increase in the giving of our churches has far more than met any increase of expense for administration. Our state is one of the largest missionary fields in our country, measuring by population, need, and opportunity, and it has come to rank third among the contributing states.

From this will be seen the importance of the new field of labor to which I was called

from Stockton.   Of course, all the results
mentioned were not accomplished during my
administration, but they have resulted from
it, and not a little of it had been achieved
while I was in office.   The way was opened
for the great change, and the foundations
were laid for the results.   It was my pleasure
to introduce Congregationalism into Buffalo,
Lysander, Cortland, and Schenectady; to
revive a defunct church in Ticonderoga; to
prepare the way for churches in Utica, Ogdensburg and other places, and to bring
back a large number of our churches which
had been drawn into the Presbyterian em-
brace.   I was also called to aid ministers in
revival work, and once, through the agency
of Rev. Dr. Beard, then the president of our
society, I was invited to hold a series of meet-
meetings in South Norwalk, Connecticut, his
native place, and a very extensive work of
grace and large additions to the church were
the results.

My correspondence was very laborious,
and the typewriter was unknown.   I rarely
spent a Sabbath at home.   But Providence
favored me with good health, and in all my
journeyings no accident befell me.   So I look
back on those nine years in New York state

as being among the most fruitful in my ministry. I received strong testimony to that effect from various quarters, and at the last meeting of the State General Association and anniversary meeting of the Home Missionary Society under my administration a very flattering recognition to that effect, presented by Rev. Prof. Tyler of Cornell University, was adopted, expressive of regret at my resignation of office. In closing the record of my work in New York, I may add, though it may savor of egotism, the following letter received while writing these "Recollections," from the present excellent and efficient secretary of the State Home Missionary Society:

SYRACUSE, N. Y., May 24, 1897.

DEAR DR. HOLBROOK: It gives me pleasure to speak of your important work as the first secretary of the New York Home Missionary Society. During your nine years of service you laid the foundation for the large work that has been built thereon in the succeeding years. Your visitation to many of the fields is still remembered by the older members of the churches, and they make affectionate inquiries after you. Your wise and kindly counsel is still bearing fruits in a number of churches, and the earnest revival sermons preached at special meetings held to aid pastors, are spoken of with much warmth by those who heard and were benefited by them.

I am sure what was felt by the Board of Trustees of the Society, of which the writer was a member, was also felt by the churches throughout the state,—that we had in our secretary a man of deep piety, of strong personality, entrenched in stalwart principles and with high ideals for the infant organization. The present secretary when going through the state is often reminded of the words of the Master: "One soweth and another reapeth. . . . other men labored, and ye are entered into their labors." While every secretary has enlarged the work, all of us have been reaping the harvest of your sowing.

While the Lord has permitted you to labor in many fields, and to gather a rich harvest in them all, I feel sure that your work as secretary of the New York Home Missionary Society has been among the most fruitful in far-reaching results. Accept hearty congratulations on added years, strength, and faculties so well preserved, and above all that God has honored you beyond most men in the rich and varied blessings scattered all through your long and useful life. Many old friends in New York State would be glad to look you in the face and grasp your hand once more. But if this is not to be we shall still cherish sweet memories, a warm interest, and hearty personal regard.

Believe me, yours very cordially,

ETHAN CURTIS.

CHAPTER XXXVIII

PORTLAND, MAINE—PREACHING IN THE WEST
CHURCH—REMOVAL TO CALIFORNIA AGAIN
—RESIDENCE IN OAKLAND—FINAL SET-
TLEMENT IN STOCKTON

At length, having reached the age of 73, I
found the labor and travel devolved on me too
great, and I decided to resign my position as
secretary, to be succeeded by a younger man.
I then supposed my active service was about
ended, and I did not anticipate again en-
gaging in the stated preaching of the gospel, much as I delighted in the work, nor
assuming again any public responsibility.
But I was mistaken, for I found God had
further service in store for me. Before
returning to California, where my wife and
I had planned to spend our closing years of
life, we visited her brother and family in Portland, Maine. While there, being asked to
supply the pulpit of the West Church in that
city for a Sabbath, I did so, and to my surprise I was invited to continue to do so indefi-
nitely, as it had then no pastor. I accepted

the call as again providential, and I entered
upon the service, which continued for about
eighteen months. I enjoyed my work there
exceedingly, and in its performance had evidence that my days of usefulness were not, as
I had supposed, at an end. The people assured me that my labors were appreciated,
and I formed a very pleasant acquaintance
with the Congregational pastors of the city.
The church was much revived, there were
additions to its membership, and it has since
had able pastors and been greatly prospered.
Portland is a delightful city, with one of the
finest harbors in the land, and our residence
there will long be remembered as one of the
pleasantest episodes in our history. While
laboring with the West Church there, I
invited Rev. Dr. Clark of the Williston
Church, the originator of the Christian Endeavor movement, to assist me in organizing
such a society there. It was, I think, the
third such in order of formation. A number
of its members afterwards joined the church
while I was there.

From Portland we removed to Oakland,
California, as we had planned to do on leaving New York State, and rejoined our circle
of relatives in that place and the city of San

Francisco across the bay. And now, surely, I might expect to settle down and end my days in *otium cum dignitate*, after my long experience in such a variety of positions in life. But no, I was still in good health, and thankful still, if the Lord should so appoint, to do a little more service in my loved employ of preaching the gospel. And so it was ordered, for I had frequent calls to supply vacant pulpits in San Francisco and the vicinity. This I did for the First Church, in San Francisco, and for two or three months for Plymouth Church, and for some little time for Olivet and for Ocean View Churches. I also supplied Union Church at San Lorenzo, near Oakland, for about twenty months. My old friend, Rev. Dr. Warren, facetiously remarked, that "I had sought to retire to private life in California, but instead had found myself plunged again into the very vortex of work."

My wife and I enjoyed our residence in the delightful city of Oakland, and its refined society, exceedingly, and while there I sought to identify myself with all the operations of our denomination in the state. I had long felt the importance of some organization in every state for the relief of aged or infirm ministers, and for the benefit of the widows and children of those who were deceased without leaving provision for their comfort and support. I had secured a society for that purpose in New York state, and I therefore did the same for California. At my suggestion the "Congregational Ministerial Relief Society of California" was formed. I served as its president for several years, and it has already accomplished its end in several cases and has now a considerable accumulated fund, that is gradually increasing.

After a few years residence in Oakland, I removed with my wife to Stockton, where our elder adopted daughter was residing, and we united with the Congregational Church, of which I had once been pastor, and were cordially welcomed by its esteemed pastor, Rev. R. H. Sink, and the survivors of our old friends.

While residing there we were permitted to celebrate our golden wedding, in 1892, the anniversary of the fiftieth year of our married life. A large company assembled at the house of our daughter to congratulate us, including not only members of the church, but other citizens, and among the rest, my old and genial friend, Rev. Dr. J. H. Warren of

San Francisco, who greatly helped to enliven the occasion.

In January, 1894, I preached my eighty-sixth birthday sermon to a large audience in the Congregational Church, a copy of which I have appended, in this volume, as a fitting conclusion of my " Recollections" of the past.

20

CHAPTER XXXIX

SEMI-CENTENNIAL OF THE DUBUQUE CHURCH

While residing in Stockton there occurred, in May, 1889, an event of very great interest to us, and of no little importance to the church in Dubuque, Iowa, of which I was the first pastor, namely, the celebration of the semi-centennial anniversary of its formation. My wife and I received a very cordial and pressing invitation to be present, accompanied by the means for defraying our traveling expenses, and a message to the effect that "we cannot celebrate without you." A full report of the exercises was subsequently published in a thick pamphlet, illustrated with engravings of the three houses of worship that had been occupied, and pictures of all the pastors. They were all present except Dr. Guernsey, who was deceased. From this report I make the following extracts:

The semi-centennial was celebrated with exercises intensely interesting and full of joy from the opening hour to the close. Great preparations had been made and great expectations were indulged, but by common consent the result exceeded all that we had hoped. The homes of the former pastors were divided by the full width of the continent, and three of them were past seventy years of age, and it was thought doubtful if they could all attend. Particular solicitude was expressed in reference to Dr. J. C. Holbrook, whose residence was on the Pacific Coast, and who was in his eighty-second year. Favorable responses soon came, Dr. Holbrook's being the second. The reception of the beloved former pastors was most hearty and affectionate.

Sunday dawned clear and beautiful, and, as the daily papers said, it was truly a great day for this historic church. From 9:45 to 10:45 was given to the Sunday-school, at which each pastor made a brief address, and each was greeted with a basket of flowers. It was a delightful and impressive hour. Then the air was fairly electric with joyous anticipations as the pastors took seats on the platform, Rev. J. C. Holbrook, D. D., Rev. Lyman Whiting, D. D., Rev. J. S. Bingham, D. D., Rev. C. E. Harrington. The incumbent gave a hearty address of welcome; then followed an original jubilee hymn, an old-time anthem with many voices of former years.

On introducing Dr. Holbrook, for twenty-one years pastor of the church from almost the beginning, the pastor proposed that the audience receive him standing. Every one rose, and as the venerable doctor stepped forward to the desk, many were moved to tears. Notwithstanding his more than eighty-one years, he is a man of remarkable vigor. He had arrived only the day before, after a six days' journey, but displayed no tokens of weariness. From the opening to the close of his sermon he moved forward with strong, clear voice and eloquence. His text was Matt. 16:3, and his theme " The Signs of the Times."

His discourse was a learned review of the hopeful indications which everywhere greet the broadening kingdom of Christ. It showed that the speaker was not a despondent, looking to other times as better than these, but that he regarded this as the best epoch in the world's history, well along toward the final conquest. His sermon showed that he had kept his heart young and fresh and his mind fully abreast with the latest scientific and religious thought of the age. Happy are the men who can thus keep the sympathies of their youth and prime and grow gracefully old! Happy are the people who can have, for years, the ministry of such a man, and who can hear from him such an address and behold in the unfaded freshness of the speaker an illustration of the blessings promised in the third verse of the first Psalm!

Then follows in the report the sermon in full.

In the afternoon the Lord's Supper was celebrated, the auditorium being filled. Dr. Holbrook and Rev. Mr. Harrington assisted in administering the rite of baptism to some new members and children, Drs. Bingham and Whiting presiding at the Lord's table, with tender and beautiful words. In the evening occurred the meeting of the Christian Endeavor Society, when Drs. Bingham and Whiting spoke. At 7:30 the house was filled to its utmost capacity, when Dr. Bingham gave an address on " Still Pressing Toward the Unattained," which was original and striking in thought and expression.

This address and others are also given in full in the report.

Rev. C. E. Harrington followed with an address on " The Heroic Age of Congregationalism." The hymn, " Onward Christian Soldiers," was sung, and with the benediction the Anniversary Day closed, whose memory will long endure.   On Monday, the pastor of the church read a historical account of the fifty years' existence of the church to another large audience. After the reading, Dr. Bacon's hymn, " O God, beneath Thy guiding hand," etc., was sung, and Dr. Whiting gave an address on " Congregationalism in History," which for striking and original expression is rarely equaled, and it was frequently interrupted with bursts of laughter and applause, its quaint humor and telling facts being irresistible.

Monday afternoon was devoted to Reminiscences which had been anticipated with much pleasure. Dr. Holbrook had been named to open the floods of memory. He began with an account of his coming to Dubuque, and held up to view the manuscript, yellow with age, which was the first sermon he preached here. The mice had devoured a part of it, and he remarked that they perhaps got as much good of it as those who heard it. There was one lady present, the only survivor of the original members of the church, who heard it[1] and another lady, the first convert under Dr. Holbrook's ministry.[2]

Dr. Holbrook told of his experiences in the East raising money for the Main-street edifice. He read a list of the Dubuque subscribers to that enterprise, and suggested

[1] She has just died at the age of eighty-four while this is being written.

[2] She is still living in Chicago, and is over ninety years of age.

that this would be a good time for those in arrears to pay up. [Great laughter.] He told of the admiring remarks that used to be made about that building, to the great merriment of those present. He read an extract from the dedicatory sermon of that church in which he predicted that Iowa would become as great as it now is. He rehearsed the story of the revivals under his ministry, and told of one revival under the preaching of Rev. John T. Avery, evangelist of Ohio. One of the converts was Mr. James Steele, who subsequently went to Oregon and took part in organizing the First Congregational church of Portland. In closing, he touched the feelings of all by saying that Dubuque would ever be dear to him; it was here he began his pastoral duties; here he began his married life, and fond memories of the past clustered thickly here. He was delighted with this reunion, and looked forward to a greater when he should meet his friends in the world to come. He expressed the hope that all of the present company might be there.

Then followed a scene long to be remembered. The pastor said that there were several "elect ladies" in the audience to whom, though they had been silent listeners, these exercises had been especially interesting. By the side of each pastor, through the years of labor, of trial, of victory, there had been a faithful companion, a sharer of burdens, and more often than the people had known, the hidden cause of the pastor's successes. In modesty, and often withdrawn from the public eye, her work had been done and she had been content with her husband's success, but he now proposed, without consulting *their* wishes in the matter, to give the people an opportunity to express for each of these noble women the sentiments

of gratitude and affection which they feel.   Thereupon
he asked Dr. Holbrook to escort Mrs. Holbrook to the
platform, which he very gladly did.   As the doctor went
down for his wife and the venerable pair came forward,
Mrs. Holbrook quietly protesting, the audience rose to
their feet and saluted her with fluttering handkerchiefs in
every part of the room ; and both Dr. and Mrs. Holbrook were seated on the platform.

Very tender reference was made to the deceased wife
of Dr. Whiting, at which he was much moved, and spoke
a few words, when the hymn, " O think of the friends
over there," was sung.   Dr. Bingham then escorted his
wife to the platform, and was followed by Rev. Mr.
Harrington with his wife, and the pastor and his wife.
After which, to the close, the meeting was open for all
present to speak, and there were volleys of questions,
laughter, and applause strangely intermixed.   Dr. Bingham had previously made some tender references to Dr.
Guernsey, deceased.

These few points are but hints of the spirit and fulness
of the meeting, which will linger long in the memory of
those who were present.   All then repaired to the front
of the building, where a photographic picture was taken,
in which two hundred and fifty faces are distinctly visible ;
the pastors and their wives and the two old ladies before
referred to were in the foreground.

On Monday evening, a grand banquet was enjoyed,
which closed the celebration.   A very fine salutatory
poem by Mrs. Ada L. Collier, an authoress of reputation,
and a member of the church, was read by her, but it is
too long to copy here, though published in full.   Several
speeches were made and papers read.   In one of the latter,

Dr. B. McClure referred to the period of the late war, 1861–65, and the attitude of this church in reference to it. He mentioned the names of members of the church who entered the army, and said among other things:

"And need I say in this presence, that the pulpit of this church gave forth no uncertain sound? There were members of this church born and bred in slave states, who held to the doctrine of state rights, so-called, and to the theory that African slavery was right, not only right but Christian; who after the delivery of a certain sermon by the then pastor, Rev. John C. Holbrook, left us, seceded and were no more with us forever. And the old bell that hung in the tower! It too was true. It tolled out its sad notes when news of defeat was brought to us; and gave forth its loudest notes of cheer when victory perched upon our banners. Its final notes of victory were too much for bell-metal to endure, and it burst its bands while ringing out its gladdest notes for liberty and union. Lee had surrendered and the *Cause* was lost—our country was saved."

Following this, there were several receptions at houses of members of the congregation, and I baptized several children of those who in early days I had admitted to the church, and of some even that I had baptized in childhood, and the grandchildren of those who long years before had been married by me.

As one of many illustrations of the civil and religious progress of our country, I may state that the *Territory* of fifty thousand people, when I crossed the Mississippi, has expanded into one of the noblest states of the middle west, with over two millions of inhabitants. The little mining town of fifteen hundred people has grown into a grand city of forty thousand inhabitants, with an extensive trade, and a network of six or more railroads in every direction, connecting with lines to the Pacific and to Mexico, to Canada, and soon will reach the *ultima thule* of our country, Alaska; while the little pastorless church of nineteen members, with a dingy, unfinished house of worship, mortgaged for more than its worth, has become one of the largest in the state, with a magnificent edifice, having colonized three times to form two Presbyterian churches and a second Congregational, and having aided in establishing a large German Congregational church, the wife of whose pastor was a member of my church.

I shall be excused, I trust, for dwelling thus on this semi-centennial celebration, since it was, to me, one of the most memorable episodes in the history of my long life-work. Dear old city, where I began my pastoral labors as a home missionary, with much self-denial, and where I spent, perhaps, my happiest years, you are enshrined in my memory! Dear old church of my first love, and my fellow laborers there, I shall through eternity rejoice in my connection with you! Many whom I loved, and many converted under my ministry, have entered the heavenly mansions, and others, with myself, are hoping to join them at no distant day. What reminiscences shall we have to recall when we all meet again in our Father's house,

> Where saints are completely blest;
> Have done with sin, and care, and woe,
> And with their Saviour rest.

Ann L. Holbrook.

CHAPTER XL

And now comes one of the saddest chapters
in all the experiences of my long life. Soon
after the celebration of the fiftieth anniversary
of our marriage, there developed in my wife
the first indications of a disease which ere long
resulted in her death. She felt from the first
that it would prove fatal, but with remarkable Christian fortitude she looked forward
to the end, her chief anxiety being on my
account. She was younger than I, and she
had often said she hoped to outlive me, and
minister to my comfort while I lived. And
such had been my prayer; but our heavenly
Father directed otherwise. Every means
available was resorted to for her relief, but
in vain. At last we went to San Francisco,
to avail ourselves of the services of a special-
ist in the line of her ailment; but the disease
baffled every effort for its removal, and, after
four years from the time it first appeared,
the end came November 20, 1896, and she

quietly fell asleep in Jesus. She had a firm trust in the Saviour, and said she should never be better prepared than then for the great change.

The last books we read together were Ian Maclaren's "Upper Room" and Dr. Dale's "Future Life," and the last hymn I read to her was that beautiful one of Keble's, which she said was one of her favorites, "Sun of my soul, thou Saviour dear," etc., and especially the verse,—

> Abide with me from morn till eve,
> For without Thee I cannot live;
> Abide with me when night is nigh,
> For without Thee I dare not die.

She was always specially interested in home and foreign missions, and while we resided in that State she secured the forma-·tion of the New York State Branch of the Woman's Board of Missions at Boston, acting as its secretary, organizing auxiliaries, and writing papers and annual reports. In Stockton she was president of the Woman's Missionary Society of the Congregational Church, and at her death a very tender memorial paper was adopted by her associates. The following is an extract:

Our hearts are sad, as we gather to-day, in missing the familiar form of our dear president, Mrs. Holbrook, and we realize how great a loss we have sustained by her death.   Her lovely Christian character, and her untiring labors in the missionary cause, have endeared her to us personally, and we feel that we have lost our most faithful and efficient member.   .   .   .   Hers was a life filled with good works, and the influence of her life and character will long be felt in the church, in this society, and in the community in which she lived.

The executive committee of the Woman's Board of Missions of the Pacific also testified to her worth and works in resolutions adopted and published in the *Pacific*.   They said:

She will be missed, not only in the domestic circle, but in the churches of California, where her faithful, loving service has left a sweet and hallowed influence.   Her earnestness, loyalty, and devotion, unostentatiously expressed, were an inspiration to the work of this Board, which now mourns her loss.   Many of us remember her earnest words and helpful suggestions at our last annual meeting.   Those of us who have had the pleasure of entertaining her in our homes can testify to her ever-ready sympathy and love for the Master's service in every act.

Her influence will abide with us ; her example we will do well to follow until we, too, are called to lay down the work which is so dear to us.

The following is an extract from a tribute to her worth written by Mrs. Ada L. Collier, the authoress, a member of the church in Dubuque, and published in one of the daily papers of that city :

Mrs. Ann Holbrook was an ideal minister's wife. Hers were the hands never idle, and the heart never empty. In the vague memories of those old days, amid the struggles and privations of an early church, the face of Mrs. Holbrook comes in view, and her silent, self-sacrificing ministry is outlined in the brightest of tints. For her ministry was as distinct and vital as was that of her distinguished husband. As an example of her entire faithfulness, it may be instanced that in twenty years' service as a Sabbath-school teacher she was never absent but one Sabbath.

She was a humble and sincere Christian, the warm friend of the friendless, and the guide of the erring. Of a joyous and even temperament, her religion was of a sunny type, and she never lost the youthfulness of heart that endeared her to the young and old alike.

She bore her last illness with a serene spirit, and without pain or murmuring passed peacefully away.

To few indeed falls so beautiful a married life as to Dr. and Mrs. Holbrook. They lived in the holiest and most tender companionship for fifty-four years. For them the "silver-wedding day" dawned softly bright; for them the "golden-marriage morning" widened and glowed into almost unearthly beauty, and for them whose hands are unclasped here, "for a little while," awaits the glad reunion in God's shadowless day.

In the quiet cemetery at Stockton, where the bland airs of the Occident blow gently, she sleeps the sleep that wraps mortality "when day is gone."

I will add an extract from an obituary notice written by a friend and published in the San Francisco *Pacific:*

Hers was an eventful and especially useful life. She was born in Farmington, Conn., December 9, 1822. Her father moved to Illinois in 1831 and settled in Jacksonville, where his name stood third on the roll of the First Church there. Mrs. Holbrook studied at Monticello Seminary, at Godfrey, Ill., the oldest institution of the kind in the West, and presided over by the Rev. Theron Baldwin, D. D., who afterwards became secretary of the Congregational College Society. About two years after her return home, she was married, in October, 1842, to Rev. J. C. Holbrook, who in the same year commenced his first pastorate at Dubuque, Ia.

Mrs. Holbrook was a very able and efficient co-laborer with her husband in his many and varied fields of activity. She had what might be termed remarkable gifts of tact, patience, and affection, united with so much simplicity and earnest though diffident resolve to do her best, that wherever she lived she had the entire love and confidence of all the people.

Mrs. Holbrook made profession of religion and united with a Congregational church in Illinois in her early girlhood, remaining thereafter a conscientious and consistent Christian, and dying in full hope of eternal life through her Redeemer. Her funeral, at Stockton, was attended by only most intimate friends, as she would herself have chosen, and Rev. R. H. Sink of that city officiated. One of her favorite hymns was sung,—John Keble's " Sun of My Soul."

And thus passed away my bosom companion of fifty-four years, the sharer of my joys and sorrows, my toils and responsibilities and successes; and I cannot forbear to testify to her faithful devotion to me, and to the work in which she so earnestly coöperated with me in the various positions which I have been called to occupy. To her counsel and help I owe, in large measure, any success I have achieved; and to her amiability and tact and good judgment, which not only averted enmities, but made warm friends, is due in good part the harmony that always existed between me and the people of my charge in the pastoral relation; and to her untiring care for my welfare is to be ascribed, no doubt, in part the lengthening out of my days so far beyond the average of human life.

For weeks I watched the ebbing tide of her life, and my sensations could not be better described than in the following lines, which have since come under my eye:

They
Who never saw the eyelids close,
Beneath whose shadowing fringes lay
All that had given to life repose,
Or charm, or hope, or ease, or joy,
Or love clear molten from alloy;
Who have not, tear-blind, watched the breath

That only breathed to bless them, come
Slower and fainter, till the dumb
  Unanswering lips grew white with death,
They cannot know, by grief untaught,
  What an unfathomed depth I find
Of ebbless anguish in the thought
  That I am left behind.

The skeptic, John Stuart Mill, as he stood in anguish beside the grave of his wife, not expecting ever again to meet her, admitted that the Christian's confident hope of reunion in the future state with those loved on earth, has, in such circumstances, an advantage that cannot be overestimated, and that "if that hope cannot be proved to be true, it certainly cannot be unproved."

And so, as Whittier says, "beside the Silent Sea I wait the muffled oar," and in my ninetieth year look for a consummation of my hopes not only in beholding the "blissful face" of the Saviour and "standing complete in righteousness," but also in meeting again the friends gone before.

So long God's power hath blest me, surely still
    'T will lead me on
Through dreary doubt, through pain and sorrow, till
    The night is gone,
And with the morn, those angel faces smile
Which I have loved long since and lost awhile.

21

Says Martineau,—" While we poor way-farers still toil, with hot and bleeding feet, along the highway and the dust of life, our companions have but mounted the divergent path, to explore the more sacred streams, and visit the diviner vales, and wander amidst the everlasting Alps, of God's upper province of creation.   And so we keep up the courage of our hearts and refresh ourselves with the memories of love and travel forward in the path of duty with less weary step, feeling ever for the hand of God, and listening for the domestic voices of the immortals whose happy welcome waits us.   Death, in short, under the Christian aspect, is but God's method of colonization; the transition from this mother country of our race to the fairer and newer world of our emigration."

Yet love will dream, and Faith will trust
That somehow, somewhere meet we must.
Alas for him who never sees
The stars shine through his cypress trees!

—*Whittier*.

"A truth learned in the hours of faith, but a truth to flesh and sense unknown."

CHAPTER XLI

CONCLUSION—DEGREE OF LL. D. CONFERRED—
IMPORTANCE OF THE NINETEENTH CENTURY
AND ITS PROGRESS—EXTRACTS FROM MY
DUBUQUE SEMI-CENTENNIAL DISCOURSE

Just as I was writing the last of the preceding chapter, I received notice that Norwich University,[1] at Northfield, Vt., my native state, had conferred on me the honorary title of LL. D. I confess my surprise, for I am sure I felt that I had little claim to such distinction, compared with multitudes of others, but I accepted it as evidence that some, at least, who had known my history, believed that I had not lived altogether in vain. It impressed me anew with a sense of my obligation to the grace of God which has enabled so poor an instrument as I have been to accomplish anything in his service, and for the benefit of his fellow men. To Him be all the glory.

To any one who has felt interest enough in the matter, and has had the patience to follow the record of my life in the foregoing pages,

[1] See Appendix.

it must be apparent that it has been an active one, and one that may be appropriately termed a *practical* one. I have written no profound theological, philosophical, or scientific work; have made no wonderful discoveries or inventions, and have achieved no literary fame, but I have *worked* faithfully to advance the Redeemer's kingdom, and I trust have done something towards that end.

It admits of serious doubt in my mind whether it would have been of advantage to me in the course marked out for *me* by Providence, had more of the early years of my manhood been spent in the halls of learning instead of among men and amid the scenes of active business life; but there can be no doubt that for the vast majority of candidates for the ministry, a thorough collegiate and theological course of education is necessary, and in some cases indispensable to the highest success. That I do not undervalue the importance of institutions of learning for that purpose is proved by the fact that I have been more or less directly or indirectly connected with the founding and support of Iowa, Beloit, and Rockford (female) colleges, and the Chicago and Pacific Theological seminaries.

In reviewing my life as I have now done, I

repeat again my thankfulness that I have lived in such a period of the world's history as is embraced in the present century.

"At no time," says Mr. John Fiske, "since men have dwelt upon the earth have their notions about the universe undergone so great a change as in the century of which we are approaching the end. Never before has knowledge increased so rapidly; never before has philosophical speculation been so actively conducted or its results so widely diffused. . . . This century is an epoch the grandeur of which dwarfs all others that can be named since the beginning of the historic period. In their mental habits, in their methods of inquiry, and in the data at their command, the men of the present day are separated from the men whose education ended in 1830 by an inestimably wider gulf than ever before divided one progressive generation of men from their predecessors. . . The great achievements of archeologists and the unearthing of ancient cities belong almost entirely to the present century. In books of logic the score of centuries between Aristotle and Whately saw less advance than between Whately and Mill. . . . The eyes of the twenty-first century will, no doubt, point back

to the age just passing away as the opening of
a new dispensation."

But wonderful as has been the advance
which has been made during this century in
the respects thus specified, and in others to
which I referred in my eighty-sixth birthday
sermon (see Appendix), yet I love to dwell
with more satisfaction on the progress that has
been made in the advancement of the kingdom of God, to which I also alluded in my
sermon just referred to. This country has
witnessed the *renascence* of the missionary
spirit in the Christian world, and more has
been accomplished in the spread of the gospel
and in preparation for its universal triumph
than was true even of the apostolic days, or
in all the centuries since, till the present one.

How remarkable have been the strides in the
work of evangelizing our own land, and how
rapid the multiplication of churches of all
denominations, and the increase of members
far beyond the proportionate increase of our
population ! To speak of our own Congregational body, how notable has been its development, and its expansion from the little
section of New England to every state and
territory in the Union, rendering it no longer

provincial but national! Instead of the few churches in the region where it was first planted, there are now nearly 6,000 churches, with over 600,000 members, with seven theological seminaries and over fifty colleges, while the contributions for the home and foreign missionary societies and their auxiliaries have swelled from a few hundred, at first, to millions annually.

The epoch under review has, also, witnessed a most encouraging development of the spirit of philanthropy and of liberality in giving not only for the relief of the suffering, but for the endowment of educational institutions, and the elevation of the degraded. The accursed system of human slavery has been abolished in our own land and in the whole civilized world. The spirit of union among Christians and the recognition of the right of toleration in religious belief and of all the other rights of man have made a marked progress beyond any other like period of history.

Perhaps I cannot better close this review than by quoting here a passage from the sermon which I preached on "The Signs of the Times," at the semi-centennial celebration of the church of which I was the first pastor in

Dubuque, Iowa. After enumerating the advantages we now possess for the spread of the gospel, I said :

So we see, that all these great systems of combined and world-wide enterprises for the renovation of society and the conversion of the world have been invented, or perhaps better inspired of God, within less than a century, and we are ready to say, What were Christians thinking about, and what were they doing previously ? But the world was not ripe for this great movement of which I speak before, nor were there the needed facilities for doing the work which we now possess.

It is not a quixotic enterprise then in which the Church is engaged of converting the world to Christianity. Compare the aspect of the world now, the progress of exploration, the improvements in the arts and all the facilities for prosecuting the work of evangelization, with those of apostolic days and tell me why, if you can, with the same zeal and self-consecration and prayer as distinguished the first Christians we should not see vastly greater results. We have the same gospel now, the same promises, the same almighty Spirit to coöperate with us, and men are to be converted in the same way now and society revolutionized as in apostolic days.

And how grand an enterprise is this in which we are engaged ! Not the extension of national power and dominion, and the achievement of worldly glory, but the spread of the kingdom of the Prince of peace, the elevation of a degraded humanity, the establishment of human rights, and the reconciliation of men to God, and their eternal salvation.

" The great Leader under whom we serve is operating with a plan. How inspiring to *detect that plan* and to coöperate with him in it ! " Celsus, an early opponent of Christianity, deemed it absurd to attempt the propagation of a universal religion. But the progress already made renders its practicability plain to sight, for all things point in one direction.

There is something sublime beyond compare in the steady onward progress of Christ's religion on earth, in spite of all obstacles and opposition. We are stirred as we read the campaigns of Alexander and Napoleon, but far more thrilling and impressive to me are the visions which by the eye of faith I see of the spiritual and moral conquests of Jesus ; kings yielding to his supremacy and nation after nation acknowledging his sway, until finally "every knee bows and every tongue confesses that he is Lord to the glory of God the Father."

> No conqueror's sword he bears,
> Nor warlike armor wears,
> Nor haughty passion stirs to conquest wild ;
> In peace and love he comes
> And gentle is his reign
> Which o'er the earth he spreads by influence mild.
>
> The peaceful Conqueror goes
> And triumphs o'er his foes,
> His weapons drawn from armories above.
> Behold the vanquished sit
> Submissive at His feet,
> And strife and hate are changed to peace and love.

Oh, I pity the man who has no sympathy with the work of the world's salvation, but is content to plod along through life immersed in worldly cares and schemes, feeling no enthusiasm to join in this great enterprise and destined to have no part in its final triumph, when angels and just men made perfect shall raise the anthem, " The kingdoms of this world are become the kingdoms of our Lord, and of his Christ ! "

Such has been the century I have described, and through most of which I have lived ; it has been a privilege, and yet I envy those who are just coming on the stage, and are to witness the developments of the next. To the eye of faith there looms up a period of still greater progress than in the past, and of more glorious displays of God's love to man, and of the power of the gospel. But I hope to look down from the heights of heaven and see the triumphs of God's grace in the redemption of this fallen world.

APPENDIX

From the San Francisco Pacific

DR. HOLBROOK'S DISCOURSE ON HIS EIGHTY-SIXTH BIRTHDAY

"I will remember the years of the right hand of the Most High" (Ps. 77 : 10).

"Bless the Lord, O my soul, and forget not all his benefits" (Ps. 103 : 2).

The Apostle Paul in one of his epistles declares that, forgetting the things which were behind, he reached forth to those which were before. And, no doubt, instead of dwelling on our past discouragements, our failures and mistakes, or even morbidly on our sins, which would tend to dishearten us, it is wiser rather to contemplate the possibilities of the future, and thus be stimulated to aspire after higher degrees of holiness and usefulness. Still, it is becoming and profitable, at stated seasons, to look back on the past and call to remembrance the manifestations of God's goodness towards us, that we may feel and express our gratitude, and have our faith and hopes strengthened.

Accordingly, on this my eighty-sixth birth-day, I have thought it might be profitable to others, as well as myself, to take a backward glance on my past history and experiences, and in the spirit of the writers of my text, to " remember the years of the right hand of the Most High," and call on my soul to " bless the Lord, and not to forget his benefits."

I. And the first benefit for which I desire to-day to bless the Lord is that I had my birth in a Christian family, and was trained under the shadow of the sanctuary, in the midst of Christian influences. From the ear-liest period of my childhood, I felt the influ-ence of pious parental example, and prayers, and instruction. The family worship regu-larly maintained, the strict observance of the Sabbath as a day of sacred rest, constant attendance on the services of God's house, and on the Sabbath-school, and the atmos-phere of a Christian community—all had a hallowed effect upon me to restrain me from forming vicious habits, and to prepare me for the never-to-be-forgotten revival of relig-ion in which I was early led to enter upon the Christian life, and which was the beginning of sixty-seven years of devotion to the service of Christ.

Who can estimate the value of such privileges and influences in the development of character and the shaping of one's destiny for time and eternity? Thousands upon thousands now in the realms of glory, and thousands upon thousands more to be added to their number, will bless God through eternity for a Christian parentage. There is an entail of religion that passes from Christian parents to their offspring of infinitely more value than wealth, however great. Better, far better, to be an heir of God than of the greatest millionaire.

It is a fact that the vast majority of those that are gathered into the churches come from Christian families, and if all professedly Christian parents were consistent in their lives, and faithful in training their households in the way they should go, it would be one of the mightiest factors in building up the kingdom of God on earth, and not second even to the preaching of the gospel.

Let me, then, urge all who have the responsibility of training children to be watchful over their own walk and conversation, and faithful in instilling into the youthful mind the principles of religion, reverence for God's house and the Sabbath, and the duty and privilege of being numbered among the disciples of Christ. Let a cheerful and consistent piety reign in the household, and let it be seen that " religion never was designed to make our pleasures less."

And, my young friends who listen to me to-day, who have Christian parents, let me impress on your minds the value of this advantage, and, if you have not already done so, let me exhort you to yield early to the influences brought to bear upon you, and to enter upon a Christian life before you shall come under those powerful counter-influences which will meet you when you go forth to face the temptations of the world. Had I not done so, how different would have been my life and my eternal destiny !

II. The second benefit for which I desire to bless God to-day is that, in the language of the apostle, he " counted me faithful, putting me into the ministry." This is the noblest and most exalted occupation of man, and after more than fifty years devoted to it, if I were to live my life over again, it would be my choice of all others. It is an occupation most favorable not only to one's own personal improvement, but also to one's usefulness to others.

The true minister of Christ is occupied with the highest possible themes of contemplation, calculated to expand his mind, enlarge his heart, and ennoble his character. What other science can compare in this respect with the science of theology? What study with the study of the Word of God? And what labor so satisfying and exhilarating as that of saving souls and building up the kingdom of God? Had I a thousand lives to live, they should all be devoted to this. And what are the rewards of any other occupation, though fame and wealth should be the result, compared with the satisfaction of having helped to prepare immortal souls for a future glorious destiny, and of having done something to make the world better, by preaching that gospel that is designed for its redemption?

If there is a young man here to-day who is considering what shall be his future course in life, and has not yet decided, let me urge him to give himself to the work of the ministry of the gospel. It is the testimony of one who has tried the experiment, and has had half a century's experience and observation, that he will never regret such a decision.

I grant and rejoice in the fact that one may be useful, and serve his God and generation in any honest calling, and in any of the walks of life, so that no one need ever live in vain. Multitudes have made themselves a blessing to the world in very humble spheres; but still it is true that it is an unequaled honor and privilege to occupy the position of a minister of Christ. As Paul declares, "If a man desire the office of a bishop [or, as the word means, a pastor], he desireth a good work."

III. Again, I bless God to-day that I have been permitted to live in the present era of the world's history. This nineteenth century is, in many respects, the most interesting and important of all the centuries since the world began. True, there have been others in which one or more events have occurred that have exerted a world-wide influence, but no century has witnessed so great advances in civilization, and such vast and rapid progress in arts and science, such discoveries in and application of the powers of nature, so many inventions calculated to benefit mankind, such manifestations of the spirit of philanthropy, and such a degree of Christian enterprise.

The ancients were proud of their so-called "seven wonders of the world"—the pyramids of Egypt, the hanging gardens of Babylon, the Pharos of Alexandria, the noble statue of Jupiter Olympus by Praxiteles, the Temple of Diana at Ephesus, the Colossus of Rhodes, and the Mausoleum of Artemesia. But what were all these in practical value compared with the almost seventy-times-seven wonders of the modern world? The steam engine, that has wrought such a revolution in mechanics, manufactures, and travel; the railroad, traversing mountain, valley, and river, and sweeping its trains with lightning speed across continents; the telegraph, enabling us to hold converse as with a neighbor with far-distant places, and even across the vast ocean; the photograph, that not only pictures for us the faces of our friends and the scenery of earth, but also presents to us the aspects of the planetary spheres, and that reveals to us thousands and millions of stars undiscernible through the most powerful telescopes; the spectroscope, that enables us to ascertain the materials of distant worlds, the adaptations of the wonderful capacities of electricity; the anæsthetics, that divest the most critical surgical operations of pain; the power printing-press, that throws off its sheets by the thousands every few minutes—each one of these, and others that might be named, is worth more to mankind than all the ancient seven wonders of the world combined. They not only enhance the material comfort and welfare of man, but they also facilitate the great work of spreading the gospel, and the upbuilding of the kingdom of God on earth. Indeed, were it not for some of these discoveries and inventions, it would not be possible to carry on the work of missions on its present scale. And this leads me to say that it is a remarkable illustration of the providence of God that this astonishing progress in material things should so exactly synchronize or coincide in time with the development of the missionary spirit in the churches. During this very century that has been distinguished by such wonderful inventions and discoveries there has been exhibited such enterprise among Protestant Christians in the work of the world's evangelization as to render this emphatically the missionary era.

It is but one hundred years since the first movement for giving the gospel to the heathen began in England, and it was not till I was two years old that the first foreign missionary society in this country was formed— our American Board of Missions, which has been followed by others in all the leading Christian denominations. I was five years old when the first missionaries sailed from this country for India, and it was with difficulty that they secured permission to land and begin their labors. Then the problem was where to find a field in which to labor— now the whole world is open to the gospel. Even Spain and Austria, the most bigoted of Roman Catholic countries, can be reached; and Italy, the very home of the Pope, has its Protestant churches, and the Bible is circulated there by thousands.

It is within my remembrance that all our great religious and philanthropic societies were organized; the Home Missionary, the Bible and Tract, the Peace, the Temperance, the Anti-Slavery, the Y. M. C. A., the Christian Endeavor societies—these, and many others, have come into being in my lifetime.

The Bible has been translated into three hundred and fifty different languages and dialects, and is being printed and circulated by millions from year to year, and Christians have been permitted to introduce the gospel into nearly every country on the globe.

Yes, the world has been growing better since I came upon the stage of life, and I rejoice that I have been permitted to witness such vast changes for the better. Never before in the annals of our race were there so many channels opened for doing good as now, and never before could any individual do so much to benefit his fellow men; never before was life so well worth living for one desirous of usefulness, never before was there so little excuse for a useless life. Why, ten years in this century were worth more than five hundred before the flood, or two hundred in the middle ages. Never before could one enjoy so much, learn so much, and do so much good as in this nineteenth century.

The first century of our era was indeed marked by the greatest event in history—the advent of our Lord Jesus Christ—and by wonderful displays of the power of the gospel in the conversion of men and the establishment of churches; but the present century has witnessed more extensive progress of the gospel in the world than the first, and far more of the spirit of philanthropy and the adoption of measures for the relief of suffering humanity.

Yes, I repeat, I am glad I have lived in this era of the world's history, and that I have been permitted to share a humble part in the progress of the world. And could I live another eighty-six years, with renewed health and strength, they should all be employed for the same great end. But my active work is done. Says Miss Frances Havergal: " I suppose nobody ever did naturally like the idea of growing older, at least after they had left school. There is a sense of oppression and depression about it. The irresistible and inevitable onward march of moments and years casts an autumn-like shadow over even many a spring birthday. But how surely the Bible gives the bright side of a fact that, without it, could not help being gloomy ! "

To the aged Christian there is increasing light—light on God's Word, light on God's providence, light on God's love and faithfulness, and the near foreshadowings of the glorious light of heaven. We should have said, "At evening there shall be shadows." God says, "At evening time it shall be light." While " the way of the wicked is as darkness," " the path of the just is as the shining light, that shineth more and more unto the perfect day."

As Miss Havergal says : " Some of the fruits of the Spirit are peculiarly characteristic of sanctified older years. Witness the splendid ripeness of Abraham's faith in old age; the grandeur of Moses' meekness when he went up into the mountain to die; the mellowness of Paul in his later epistles, and the gentleness of John that makes us forget he was once a son of thunder."

The old Christian who has had a lifelong experience of the faithfulness of God to His promises, how can he doubt that He will be faithful to the end! "Even to your old age I am he," says God; "and even to hoar hairs will I carry you." We shall always be His little children, and He will always be our Father.

> Fear not the westering shadows,
>   O children of the day!
> For brighter still and brighter
>   Shall be your homeward way:
> Resplendent as the morning,
>   With fuller glow and power,
> And clearer than the noonday,
>   Shall be your evening hour.

And now, before I close, let me bear my testimony to some important points. First, I am a living witness to the truth of Solomon's declaration, that religion promotes health and long life: and of the assertion of the apostle, that "Godliness has the promise of the life that now is as well as of that which is to

come." I have never been addicted to the
use of tobacco or intoxicating drinks, which
undermine and destroy the health of so many.
These, with licentiousness, overtaxing the
system in the pursuit of wealth and the objects
of ambition, neglect of the Sabbath, and failure to cultivate the religious and moral nature,
all tend to shorten life, and religion guards
against these foes of man. If all men obeyed
the laws of God the average length of human
life would be vastly increased.

Again, I can testify, after more than sixty
years' experience, that the Christian life is the
most useful life. Not only does it guard one
from exerting a baleful influence on society,
but it brings him into coöperation with others
in every good work, and makes him a partici-
pator in innumerable measures that are
designed and adapted to elevate society,
promote good morals, and fit men for a
blessed immortality; and by his godly and
consistent example, he commends his religion
to his fellow men, and leaves behind him an
influence that will work on after he is dead
and gone.

Astronomers tell us there are stars so far
distant from us that it takes years for their
light to reach the earth, and if they were sud-

. denly blotted out, the light that is on its way to us would not reach us for a quarter of a century; or as Whittier says,—

> Were a star quenched on high
> For ages would its light,
> Still trembling downward from the sky,
> Fall on our mortal sight.
> So when a good man dies:
> For years beyond our ken,
> The light he leaves behind him lies
> Along the paths of men."

I can also testify that a Christian life is a happy life. As Solomon says, Wisdom's "ways are ways of pleasantness, and all her paths are peace." Old Jacob, at the age of one hundred and thirty years, told Pharaoh, "Few and evil have the days of the years of my life been"; and the author of Psalm xc declares, "The days of our years are three score years and ten; and if by reason of strength they be four score years, yet is their strength labor and sorrow."

But this has not been my experience. I have had my share of trials, and some of them severe, but my blessings have been a thousand times more, and I can clearly see, as I look back (and this is one of the advantages of age), that my trials have all been "blessings in disguise." I can perceive now clearly that they have resulted not only in my personal improvement, but that they were indispensable to my greatest usefulness. It is clear as day to me now that, as Cowper says,—

> The clouds ye so much dread
> Are big with mercies, and will break
> In blessings on your head.

I believe with Paul, that "these light afflictions, which are but for a moment, work out for us a far more exceeding and eternal weight of glory."

And finally, I am fully convinced, from my own long experience and observation, that there is a special providence of God in all the affairs of men. This is clearly revealed in Scripture, and it has been many times illustrated in my life. As I look back I can see that God has "led me in a way that I knew not."

How often have my plans been thwarted for the best! How often has God interposed to protect me from danger and from sin! How often has he unexpectedly opened up to me opportunities for usefulness! How often upheld me in trials! How often helped me to meet responsibilities! How often provided for my wants when in straits! I have been young, and now am old, yet have I never been forsaken nor compelled to beg bread. Believe me, my hearers, young and old, it is safe to trust God in all the scenes and circumstances of life. "They that trust in the Lord shall be as Mount Zion, which cannot be moved."

As I look back to-day on eighty-six years on earth, I can most heartily adopt the beautiful lines of the immortal Addison, who, on his death-bed, sent for a skeptical neighboring nobleman to come and see in what peace a Christian can die:

> When all thy mercies, O my God,
>   My rising soul surveys,
> Transported with the view, I 'm lost
>   In wonder, love and praise.
>
> Unnumbered comforts on my soul
>   Thy tender care bestowed
> Before my infant heart conceived
>   From whence those comforts flowed.
>
> When, in the slippery paths of youth,
>   With heedless steps I ran,
> Thine arm unseen conveyed me safe,
>   And led me up to man.
>
> Thy bounteous hand, with worldly bliss,
>   Has made my cup run o'er;

And, in a kind and faithful friend,
  Has doubled all my store.

Ten thousand thousand precious gifts
  My daily thanks employ,
Nor is the least a grateful heart
  That tastes those gifts with joy.

Through every period of my life
  Thy goodness I 'll pursue,
And after death, in distant worlds,
  The glorious theme renew.

Through all eternity, to Thee
  A joyful song I 'll raise ;
For oh, eternity 's too short
  To utter all thy praise !

BRIEF SKETCH OF NORWICH UNIVERSITY

The following extracts from the catalogue of Norwich University will give an idea of its importance:

This institution was founded in 1819 by Capt. Alden Partridge, of whom a cut appears in this book, and was known as the American Literary, Scientific and Military Academy. It retained the name until November 6, 1834, when a charter of incorporation was granted it by the state of Vermont, under the name of Norwich University.

Thus was founded the *first* scientific, classical, and military college in the United States. This new departure met with universal favor, and its halls were soon crowded with young men from every state in the Union.

In March, 1866, the university buildings at Norwich were destroyed by fire, and the university was removed to Northfield, Vermont, where the citizens had offered fine grounds and commodious barracks. Here the same system of instruction and military discipline is maintained, and many young

www.ingramcontent.com/pod-product-compliance
Lightning Source LLC
Chambersburg PA
CBHW051124120726
47905CB00005B/1413